KEEPING SHILOH

Book One

By: Ashleigh Meyer

CHAPTER 1

Jude brought the Jeep to a stop in a narrow parking space between the library and a community garden. Still buckled, she craned her neck to look up at the vinyl banner strung between light posts over the street. "End of Summer Spectacular," she read aloud. From her seat she could see McGrew's Antiques N' Things, a cafe advertising an ambitious list of homemade pies, and a fire department sign that read "Everyone's Invited to Ella May's 98th BDay - August 4th." Jude took a long, deliberate breath and glanced at Shiloh in the rearview mirror. "Are you sure about this?" she asked.

The three-year-old blinked back wide-eyed and nodded, pulling at her car-seat straps. Reluctantly, Jude got out of the car and walked around to unbuckle her.

They'd noticed the farmer's market the weekend before, on their second day in town. When talking about possible Saturday activities, Jude made the mistake of mentioning it to Shiloh, and she woke up ready and eager. She'd been cooped up inside all week and deserved a little fun. And as much as Jude hated small town charm, she knew she'd have to get used to it. Plus, they'd run out of food at home and needed groceries.

Acadia was a large, rural county with a very small town at the center, surrounded on all sides by mountains. The buildings, all made of faded old bricks and hand-carved moulding, were no more than three stories tall. It was one of those charming, quaint places with ribbons on every street light, and rock-a-thons and bluegrass festivals every weekend. It was a place very different from Brooklyn, New York, where Jude grew up. But it was not all that different from Gideon's hometown in Indiana, where she'd lived for nearly four years prior, and Jude had come to know small towns. She liked the quiet. No street noise, no mobs of tourists. But there was also no privacy. In Brooklyn she couldn't step outside her apartment without running into 6 strangers before she made it to the street. But there was a unique privacy in being surrounded by strangers; eye contact was the most intimate exchange she could expect, and it was rare. Not like in small towns. People stop, people talk, people get to know you. They shake your hand and pat your back and ask probing questions. All of these things made Jude's skin crawl and elevated her anxieties.

It seemed all the residents of Acadia were milling around the outdoor market. There were booths and stalls, a man making balloon animals, and a family selling puppies out of the bed of their pickup truck. As soon as she spotted them, Shiloh took off for the puppies and Jude bolted to keep up with her. By the time she got to the truck, Shiloh was already situated on the tailgate with one of them in her lap; some kind of floppy-eared hound puppy with droopy eyes and big paws, falling asleep in Shiloh's arms. Jude had to pry her away, promising that they would come back and visit once more before going home.

For sale at the market was every kind of produce imaginable, all from different family farms and orchards. There was an assortment of jams and homemade honey, butter and bread, even a local cattle farmer selling butchered meat. Maybe there would be no need to go to the grocery store at all. Jude made a few purchases: carrots, potatoes, strawberry jam. Shiloh eagerly tugged at her sleeve, begging for a balloon animal, and as soon as Jude paid the farmer, she walked with Shiloh to the balloon man.

"Well, hello little girl," he said, in a slobbery cartoon voice.

Shiloh beamed up at him. "I like your costume."

"Costume? What costume?" asked the clown. "I think I know what you need." He pulled two uninflated balloons out of his sleeve and blew them up, one pink, one green, then twisted the two together into the shape of a flower, and handed it to Shiloh.

Jude thanked the man and dropped two dollars into his tip jar while Shiloh marveled at the balloon.

The clown winked at Jude and said, "No, thank you. I love it when pretty girls come to visit me."

Jude laughed awkwardly. She'd never been hit on by a clown, but her love life was at an all time low so she gladly accepted and offered him a coy smile before pulling Shiloh in the other direction.

While Jude was examining some peaches, someone came up behind her and tapped her on the shoulder. She cautiously turned around, tightening her grip on Shiloh's hand.

"Well, hello!" said a bubbly woman, a little too loudly. "Oh, it's so nice to finally see you out and about! I hope you are settlin' in nicely here!"

The woman was plump and in her fifties. She wore a flower covered cotton dress down to her ankles and a yellow sun hat with one of those huge floppy brims. Her face was painted with make-up a little too bright and Jude had never seen her before. Perhaps she was evil.

"Um, I'm sorry, but have we met?" Jude asked this woman who seemed to know her. Already on the defensive, she pushed Shiloh behind her leg.

"Oh my goodness," said the woman with a bouncy laugh. "Sometimes I get ahead of myself. My name is Doris Overstreet. I am on the Welcoming Committee!"

Jude exhaled and loosened her grip on Shiloh, but didn't let go.

"I left that basket of goodies on your porch. Did

ya like it?" She leaned in close and dropped her voice to a whisper. "You're not one of them vegans, are ya?"

Jude paused for a moment. She remembered finding a basket on the front porch a few days ago. She had been in the shower and didn't hear the door. By the time she had found the basket, it was soaked from rain. There were homemade baked goods inside, all of which had become soggy and waterlogged. Not to mention that Jude was wary of random gifts landing mysteriously by her door. The basket had gone quickly from the porch to the trash.

"Oh no, not a vegan. It was great, thanks so much."

She was about to turn back to the peaches when Shiloh stepped out from behind her and smiled. "Hello," she said happily, with one arm wrapped around Jude's right leg.

Doris looked down and in her bubbly Southern voice she said, "Well, heavens, aren't you the cutest thing!"

Jude smiled briefly and began to speak, anxious to bail out of the small talk. "Well, we'd better get going. Thanks aga-"

"Now, darlin," interrupted Doris. "Where are you from? It's not very often we get newcomers around here!" She let out an over-the-top laugh and placed one hand on her bulging hip.

Apparently, escape was not going to be that easy. She dropped the peach and exhaled. This was bound to happen eventually. A crowd of locals formed around them and they all eagerly awaited her answer.

"Uh," Jude stammered. She really hadn't formulated a cohesive story yet. To explain away the slight Northern accent she carried, she began with the truth. A risky but calculated move. "We're from New York. Brooklyn, actually."

Several eyebrows lifted, a couple people looked impressed. Some guy in overalls mumbled something about *damn yankees* and walked away from the crowd. Another skinny old man in the back spat a copper-colored liquid onto the pavement. "What brought you all the way out here?" he asked.

Jude looked around at the crowd. "Well, we were just ready for a change. I grew up in the city, and thought Shiloh might be better suited someplace safer." *Safer. Yeah, right.*

"Well did you have family here or somethin'?" asked the old man.

"Um, no, no family."

"Oh, how adventurous," said Doris. "We're so happy to have you both here!" She looked down at Shiloh. "Sugar, how old are you?"

Shiloh held up her bony fingers. "Almost four!"

Doris smiled and looked back at Jude. "She's a smart one," she said. Her timbre dropped. "Sweetheart, you can't be a day over twenty."

Jude felt like she was being interrogated. All that was missing was stale coffee and a flickering fluorescent light. "I'm actually twenty three," Jude answered quickly. She was a young twenty-three. Her birthday had been just a few days before moving to town. She had a slight frame and her facial features had never really hollowed out, so she was often suspected of being much younger.

While the townsfolk all asked multiple questions at once, Jude looked off into the crowd and caught the eye of a man standing in front of a produce stall who appeared to be staring at her. He was tall and slender, with dark, messy hair and glasses, and a stack of papers and books under his arm. He wore a dark red button-up shirt tucked into his black pants, and he stood out where most others were wearing dirty blue jeans and baseball caps. He had been talking with some people, but his gaze lingered on Jude for just a moment when their eyes met. He glanced at Doris, back at Jude, then back to the couple he was talking with, but he seemed frazzled. He shifted the books in his arms and ran his free hand through the wave of hair that fell into his eyes. She watched him pat the man he'd been speaking with on the shoulder and look briefly back at her, but when he saw that she still had her eye on him, he looked quickly away.

"Honey, did you hear me?"

Jude turned her head back to Doris to see that everyone was quiet.

"Um, no, I'm sorry I didn't."

Doris laughed. "I was just wondering if your husband is around. We would love to meet him."

Jude opened her mouth to speak, but nothing came out. This woman had to know she wasn't married. She wasn't wearing a ring and she apparently looked twenty years old. She felt her neck get hot and clammy. This was what she hated about small towns, what made her nervous about them. Fake smiles and curious crowds, pointed questions punching holes in her story like swiss cheese.

"Mrs. Overstreet!" someone yelled just in time to save Jude from stammering.

When she looked, Jude saw the man in the red shirt waving and coming closer. He pushed his way up to Doris and placed a hand on her shoulder. When he did, he gave Jude a quick smile, then looked back at Doris.

"Mrs. Overstreet, I'm glad I caught you," he said. He had a deep voice and spoke swiftly, with a barely detectable stutter. Jude couldn't help but notice that, up close, he was staggeringly good-looking. He had a boyish smile and dark emerald eyes, and the faintest impression of stubble peppering his square jawline. "I've got those flyers for you. The ones Father Trent printed up for the festival." He opened a large book that had been under his arm and pulled out a stack of printed flyers. He handed them over to Doris with a quick nod.

"Oh, thank you precious," said Doris. "Oh, Christopher, I want you to meet our newest resident." She looked back at Jude. "Honey, this is Christopher. He's new to town, too, only moved in last year. He's workin' for Father Trent down at St. Mary's. It's just across the street from the Winn-Dixie. Oh, you should come on Sunday, we're havin' a revival! Anyway, Christopher, this is Jude. Just moved here with her daughter from New York. She's livin' up in the old Wesley place."

Jude recoiled when Doris told the random stranger where she lived. It was unsettling enough how much Doris knew about Jude without actually hearing it from Jude. Like her name, for starters.

He looked at her, smiled and tipped his head in her direction.That loose strand of hair fell into his eyes again and he left it there. "Nice to meet you," he said quickly. His voice had a certain nervousness about it, but he stuck out his hand.

His handshake was strong and oddly personal, and his green eyes met hers with marked interest. It wasn't a flirtatious gaze necessarily, but there was something there. He looked into her like he knew something. Like he could see something deep down.

She was startled by it, but didn't look away.

"Yeah, you too," Jude answered succinctly.

He turned back to Doris after a distinct squeeze of Jude's hand. "Well, Mrs. Doris I'll see ya on Sunday." Without saying anything, he glanced back at Jude grinning and gave her a quick nod.

"Oh, hold on a sec, I wanted to talk to you about the potluck," Doris squawked, following on his heels. "I checked the sign-up sheet. We only got three names and two of 'em are bringing corn bread. We gotta get these people motivated, honey." She grabbed him by the arm and pulled him away from the crowd. "It was great talkin' to ya' darlin'," she called back to Jude. "St. Mary's this Sunday. Havin' a big revival and potluck after. Plenty of cornbread!" she laughed. "Don't be a stranger!"

Christopher looked over his shoulder at Jude as Doris talked his ear off and pulled him through the parking lot. She watched him walk away and pulled Shiloh closer. Something about him piqued her curiosity.

When Doris left, the crowd went with her, like she was their spokeswoman.

Jude stood planted on the sidewalk for a minute, catching her breath. Once she did, she looked down at Shiloh. "This is all your fault," she stated.

Back in the Jeep, Jude heard her phone beeping and she realized that she had left it in the cup holder. She swiped the screen and read, "One Missed Call: Gideon." It beeped again, telling her that he had left a message, but she ignored it and tossed it onto the passenger seat. On the way home, they swung by a grocery store where no one bothered them and the cashier was a rude and uninterested high school student. Just what she had hoped for.

CHAPTER 2

By the time they pulled onto their gravel street, Shiloh was sound asleep. Jude had hopes of carrying her inside and putting her to bed for an hour or two so she could get some unpacking done. The farmhouse was built in 1880, and had white wood siding and plaster walls, red shutters and a red tin roof. It sat on top of a hill below the rolling Blue Ridge Mountains at the end of a winding driveway. There was only one other house visible from the yard, and it was all the way on the other side of a horse pasture. It was much larger than anything Jude had ever lived in before, and the Synedrion did their best to fill it with furniture and all of the essentials, but left boxes unpacked, thinking that Jude would want to set it up herself. Really, she wished they'd just finished the job. She wasn't one for decorating.

When the house came into view, she noticed someone standing on the porch. As she drove closer, she realized that the person was a girl, very thin, smiling softly, and appeared harmless. She was probably another townie on the Welcoming Committee. But if there was one thing Jude learned from all her training, it was that looks can be deceiving.

Glancing back at Shiloh, Jude put the car in park. The girl on the porch was watching them, and raised her arm in a small wave. She had a large duffle bag next to her at her feet. Opting to leave Shiloh in the car, Jude removed the keys from the ignition, put them in her pocket and headed for the house. As she walked, she considered the position of the small folding knife clipped to her belt. As Jude got closer to the house, the girl stepped forward to meet her, unthreatening.

"Can I help you?" Jude asked tonelessly, eyes narrowed. Her feet were planted on the sidewalk and already she was calculating the distance to Shiloh.

"Yeah, I'm Ezra. You must be Jude. It's nice to finally meet you," answered the stranger in a girlish voice. She stuck out her hand and took a step forward. Jude took a step back instinctively and crossed her arms over her chest.

She was young, probably younger than Jude. She had skin the color of chocolate milk and dark, oaky hair that sprung out everywhere in tight curls. She was strikingly pretty, unassuming, and small in every way, with high cheekbones that met her round, chestnut eyes when she smiled.

Still, Jude was a little tired of people knowing her name before she met them. "Yeah, who are you?" she asked impatiently.

Ezra looked puzzled and suddenly very nervous. "They told me that you would be expecting me."

"Who told you?"

"The Synedrion. They sent me here."

The word *Synedrion,* uttered so unceremoniously, went off like a gunshot fired from the quiet voice of a stranger and richoched around in Jude's chest. Instinctively, she glanced around to be sure no one had heard, but of course no one else was around. No one knew about the Synedrion. It was a tiny, cloak-and-dagger organization steeped in folklore and barely more than legend. They orchestrated Jude's destiny and even she barely knew who or what they were. The perceived threat had become more alarming. Jude placed her right hand over the knife at her belt without drawing attention to it. "What are you talking about," she asked, stepping forward. "Who from the Synedrion sent you and why?"

The girl stepped back and very real fear drew across her face. "Um-" She stammered. "Maxwell. Martin Maxwell."

Jude tried to be rational. Martin Maxwell was a familiar name. Maybe he was Synedrion. Maybe located somewhere in the deep South. Jude had never met him; there were only a few Synedrion officials in the United states, though more had migrated back when Shiloh was born.

Synedrion or not, no one mentioned anything to her about a pretty young Synedrion girl swinging by for a visit. Everything about this scenario seemed suspicious. She glanced back at the car to see that everything was just as she'd left it. Then, she remembered the missed call from Gideon; a Synedrion member himself.

"Okay," Jude said sternly, processing her options. "Stay right there. Don't move." When Ezra eagerly agreed, she walked back to the car, keeping one eye on the girl behind her. Shiloh was still sound asleep in her car-seat when Jude opened the passenger door. She found her phone, having slid down to the floor on the drive, and picked it up. She checked her voicemail, and sure enough, there was a message from Gideon.

"Jude, I'm sorry I couldn't inform you sooner, but I just found out myself," he said, in his usual calm, unhurried voice. "The Synedrion has decided that you could use some help. To be honest, I don't disagree." Jude pictured him sitting at his coffee table, leaning forward and rubbing the back of his neck like he always did when he was saying something he knew Jude wouldn't want to hear. "They are sending a girl your way. Her name is Ezra Lareau. She should be arriving today or tomorrow. She will be someone to train with and help you keep an eye on Shiloh. She was practically raised by the Synedrion, so you don't need to worry about keeping secrets. She knows who you are." He paused a moment. "Don't scare her off, Jude," he said quietly. "You *do* need someone. It may take some time, but you'll adjust. If you need anything, give me a call. We'll talk soon." And then he hung up.

He sounded his usual self, not like someone who was being coerced at knife point or anything. Jude stayed by the Jeep and called to the girl. "What's your last name?"

"Lareau," she yelled back, confirming Gideon's message.

Jude shook her head in amusement and frustration, picked up her sleeping child and walked back to the house. "Come in," she told Ezra as she walked past.

Once inside, Jude laid Shiloh down on the couch and covered her with an afghan. She had stirred a little on the walk from the car, but not much. When Shiloh was settled and the doors were locked, Jude led Ezra into the kitchen. She sat down at the kitchen table and suggested that Ezra join her. Gideon's words echoed in her mind. *"Don't scare her off."* Was she really that scary? Really, she looked a lot meaner than she was. First impressions were not her strong suit. Never had been. She put her elbows on the table and rested her face in her hands for a second, rubbing her eyes.

"Sorry about the interrogation," said Jude when she looked up again. "I missed the call to tell me you were coming."

"It's no problem," replied Ezra. "I understand."

Jude picked at the table cloth. “So, where are you from?” She was terrible at making small talk, but she knew Gideon was right. She did need help. And the house was too big for two people. Too much empty space made her nervous. An extra set of eyes on Shiloh could only help.

“Louisiana,” answered Ezra with a half-smile. “A town called Lafayette, south west of New Orleans.”

Jude nodded.

“How about you?”

“Brooklyn,” answered Jude as dryly as possible. “But that was a long time ago.”

Ezra nodded.

“You want some coffee?” Jude asked, already standing and going for the can.

“Coffee would be great.”

Jude began to brew a pot and peeked into the living room to check on Shiloh. She was still sound asleep.

An awkward silence permeated the kitchen and Jude placed two mugs on the table. “So…” she began. “How did you get involved in all of this?” She raised her arms to encompass all that had become her life; the house, this town, the eminent and unstoppable approach of death and danger around every corner.

"Well," Ezra began slowly. "I was orphaned when I was eight. No one wanted to adopt an unruly, half grown kid, so I became a ward of the state."

Jude couldn't picture this girl being unruly. Jude was unruly, so she knew how to identify it. Ezra was lanky, weighed maybe 90 pounds, and didn't move much at all when she spoke. Her hands were folded comfortably on the table in front of her. She spoke like she was older than she was, with a soft, easy cadence and a thick, sultry accent that Jude had never heard before.

"So I lived in girls homes and in foster care," she continued. "Until I was about thirteen. At that time, Maxwell came to see me at this group home I was living in. He asked me if I wanted to learn about my family. He told me that I had some kind of calling, and offered to take me in. It sounded better than where I was, so I went with him. From that time on, I learned about the Synedrion, and who my grandfather had been, and who I could be. I learned about you."

Jude listened to the coffee brewing and remembered her first interactions with the Synedrion. They weren't exactly positive, and she had been a much less willing participant. They had been watching her for months, tracking her movements, learning her routines, witnessing her downward spiral. On the day that she was put on academic probation at NYU, two men dressed in black suits approached her and told her that she had some great destiny. She brushed them off, even wondered if she hadn't been hallucinating. A few weeks later, Jude dropped out of NYU, and on the same day, they drugged her and took her to Gideon. Within days, her past had been wiped away, friends convinced that she had left town, and what little family she had believing the same. They'd typed a note on her computer, stating simply that she was running away and didn't want to be found. No one came looking and it really was just that easy.

"How old are you?" Jude asked.

"Nineteen," Ezra answered hesitantly. "But I'll be twenty in four months."

"Wow," answered Jude, almost accidentally.

"I know, it seems young, but I promise I can handle it." She spoke quickly, suddenly unsure of herself.

"No, it's not that," Jude answered. "I'm sure you're qualified. The Synedrion wouldn't settle for anything less."

Jude poured two cups of coffee and rejoined Ezra at the table.

"How old are you?" Ezra asked.

"Twenty three," she answered for the second time that day as she spooned way too much sugar into her coffee. Ezra turned the sugar down. "So, you learned about me," Jude said, surprised. "You know who I am?"

Ezra offered a tight smile. "Yeah," she answered after swallowing a sip of her black coffee. "It must be weird to meet someone who already knows who you are. Especially when who you are is someone that most people wouldn't believe."

Jude nodded in agreement. "I can't even tell you," she answered.

The two of them sat quietly in the kitchen for a moment, in some silent understanding. If Ezra knew about her, she probably knew that Jude too was a parentless girl. She knew that Jude too had been approached by the Synedrion with life altering news. She too had been swept up, away from a life that she knew. A life that really wasn't going anywhere. She knew who Shiloh was; why she mattered.

"I know you need to protect her," Ezra spoke, breaking the silence and glancing into the living room. "All I want to do is help. In any way that I can."

Jude turned her eyes down toward the table. Another young life destined to be short lived. "Thanks," Jude whispered, suddenly somewhere dark and unfair.

Ezra studied Jude, the mother of the child everyone in the Synedrion spoke about. The woman who was now the legend she had read about in old, dusty books with flaking covers and threadbare bindings, tucked away in secret libraries

. But she didn't look like a mother at all. Certainly not a legend. Her black tank top was too big, and she was too young. She was taller than Ezra and fair skinned, with a small frame, too thin, and had long, bright blonde hair wisping out of the disheveled bun she kept it in. She was pretty, in a subtle, careless kind of way, and wore no makeup. Her features were feminine: high cheekbones and thin, tapering lips that were pale pink and slightly bitten. Her long arms showed sculpted muscles formed not from free-spirited YMCA workouts with friends, but instead from hours of intense training, borne out of necessity and raw determination to fight. She had a willowy voice that cracked a little, like her throat was dry. But her eyes were by far her most striking feature. She had almond-shaped, fiery blue eyes that seemed far away, looking into something farther, much deeper and darker and colder than the present.

"So, I guess you'll be staying with us?" Jude asked, looking into her nearly empty coffee cup.

"If that's okay," Ezra answered. "Apparently you weren't exactly expecting me."

"It's okay," answered Jude. "This house is too big for the two of us. There's an extra bedroom upstairs. It's yours if you want it."

Ezra smiled wide, truly grateful.

A few seconds later, Jude heard the familiar sound of small bare feet on hardwood floor. She turned to see a yawning, disheveled Shiloh, dragging the afghan on the floor behind her.

She rubbed her eyes and climbed into Jude's lap. "Who are you?" she asked, looking at Ezra.

Jude laughed at her mini-me. Ezra stuck out her hand across the table like she was meeting an adult, and Shiloh shook it like she was one. "I'm Ezra. It's nice to meet you. What's your name?" she asked, though she already knew.

"Shiloh," answered the child.

"Ezra's going to be living here too," Jude said, running her fingers through Shiloh's matted hair. Ezra watched from across the table as all of Jude's sharp edges melted away, replaced with soft adoration and affection.

Shiloh nodded, picked up Jude's coffee cup and took a sip. She swallowed it down, waited a moment, made a sour face and pushed the cup away. "Yea, that's what I thought," Jude commented.

Ezra tried not to stare at the two girls in front of her. "I can't get over how much the two of you look alike," she said finally. "I mean, I guess I knew you would, but seeing it in person..."

"Yeah, it's pretty hard to deny," answered Jude. And it truly was incredible. Their physical features were more alike than most child-parent relationships. There were plenty of subtle differences, but DNA doesn't lie. Shiloh was small, and sunkissed blonde with big blue eyes. She had the same facial structure as Jude, though softer, and even the same way of holding her head when she sat at the table. Beyond the physical, however there were many differences. Shiloh shared Jude's boldness and attention to detail, but she lacked her mother's fragile temper and impulsivity. Shiloh was the picture of stillness and grace, even at four years old. She was tender and elegant, with immense capacity for compassion and focus. Some of that, no doubt, was due to her larger-than-life destiny.

Jude showed Ezra to the second bedroom upstairs, across the hall from her own.

"Sorry, the floorboards are a little wobbly," Jude told her as they climbed the creaky stairs and Jude noticed the slight tilt in the upper floor for the hundredth time. "The place is old."

"I kind of like it," Ezra answered. They stepped into her room, which was painted a soft yellow and full of sunlight that poured in from the three large windows. Jude actually liked this room the most, but her room was bigger, and she shared it with Shiloh. She was unwilling to let Shiloh sleep alone.

Ezra unpacked the few belongings she had in her bag, which consisted largely of paperback mysteries, a few articles of clothing and some crystals and strange nick-nacks that made Jude think of Gideon, who kept odd items all over his house. The rest of her things were on their way, sent from Maxwell by mail. Still, Ezra found cause to linger for most of the afternoon in her room. Neither she nor Jude were particularly outgoing, so all of their interactions were awkward and mostly avoided.

Downstairs, Jude did some unpacking of her own, with the help of Shiloh. They pulled out pots and pans, silverware, and a set of ceramic plates from the boxes in the kitchen. A table lamp, a few hardback books, throw blankets and generic artwork from the boxes in the living room. Jude let Shiloh dictate most of the decorating. And at the end of the day, despite having a refrigerator full of groceries from the market and all the kitchen gadgets one could hope for, Jude ordered a pizza for dinner. They all ate quietly on the couch with the TV on, and went to bed early.

She woke up a few hours later in a cold sweat to a loud crash of thunder. Startled, she sat straight up in bed, gasping for air. She looked around her dark bedroom, rested her right hand over her pounding heart, and caught her breath. She had been having a nightmare in which something was after her, something dark and ancient. But instead of fighting it like she would in the present, the setting was her old life in New York. Before she knew she was someone who could fight monsters.

Once her heart rate slowed and she convinced herself that it was just a dream, Jude slipped out of bed to close the window. When she had fallen asleep, the smell of Magnolia whispered through the lace curtains, carried by a warm, comforting breeze. Now, it was raining heavily and a strong wind was blowing the curtains back into the room, casting unsettling shadows across the scuffed, uneven wood floor. She shuffled across the room and pulled the window down slowly, trying not to make any noise. As the glass moved past her face, she caught a glimpse of herself in it. Her long, light blonde hair was a mess, falling out of the loose bun at the back of her head, and even in the faint reflection, her blue eyes looked tired. Not tired because she had just woken from sleep, but rather they reflected a more permanent state of exhaustion. One that, in some form or another, she had never been able to overcome. She locked the window and pulled the curtain to cover the glass. Just as she was turning for her bed, she heard a small voice call for her from across the room.

Following the sound of her daughter's voice in the darkness, Jude crossed the room to the other side where Shiloh's bed was pressed up against the wall. Shiloh was buried in covers up to her eyes. "Hey you," Jude whispered back as she sat down on the flowered quilt. "Why aren't you asleep?"

"The thunder woke me up," said Shiloh, her hair matted down from sleepy sweat. She wriggled out of the covers and into Jude's arms.

"Yeah, me too," replied Jude. At that moment there was a bright flash of lightning. Silently, Jude began counting, just like her father did with her during a storm. After 7 seconds, a crash of thunder shook the house. Shiloh jumped at the sound and buried her face in Jude's neck. "It's okay," she whispered, slowly rocking the child. "The storm's almost passed."

Without lifting her head, Shiloh mumbled into Jude's neck. "Can I come sleep with you?"

They slept in the same room, not ten feet apart, but still, Jude agreed and carried her to the larger bed across the room. Shiloh snuggled closely at Jude's side and eventually, under the cool bed sheet, the night became still.

Shiloh drifted back to sleep to Jude's soft voice humming *Dream A Little Dream Of Me.* Jude ran her fingers through her daughter's hair. She felt so soft and warm and small curled up at Jude's side and Jude lingered in the comfort of closeness. As Shiloh's breath became slow, Jude's mind wandered back to the dream she had before. It was the first time in a long time that she had really thought of New York. Usually, she wrestled with herself to block such thoughts; not that there was much to think of. She was impressed with how accurately her uninhibited dream mind had recreated her college apartment. Everything was in its place, down to the books on the shelf.

As she laid there half-heartedly trying to fall back to sleep, Jude allowed herself a few indulgent moments to think about those times. It was not quite four years ago, but seemed like centuries. It was another life entirely, and hard to believe it had ever existed. It was pre-destiny, pre-Acadia, pre-Shiloh. Life was simple, and passing by in a haze of caffeine and alcohol, late nights and microwave noodles. She saw each day only as it came and had no reason to concern herself with the idea that there may be more to life. Her parents died when she was seventeen, sending her entire world into chaos. She had never been a dedicated student, or a particularly sunny kid, but in college, she was worse than a slacker, and completely uncommitted despite her scholarship. She was damaged by trade, self-medicated and angry. She was alone and wandering, skipping classes just to sit in her apartment and do nothing.

Gideon, the man who changed everything for her, had once said that destiny begins at birth. That everything in her life had always been leading up to this: her calling. At times, Jude found this idea outrageous. Some of the events in her young life had been merely the result of happenstance and bad luck. However, there were also times when everything was perfectly clear. Her life had been set in motion years ago, before she knew how to stop it. She was on the path before she knew there was a path under her feet.

Jude pulled Shiloh closer and closed her eyes. Thoughts and images flooded over her, until she found herself back at Gideon's house in Indiana nearly four years before, meeting Shiloh for the first time. Shiloh, not yet named, was in the front doorway, in a stranger's arms. It had only been a week after meeting Gideon, and listening to him spout on about some destiny and bloodline. Honestly, she thought he was insane. But when she saw the infant that she was to call her own, the feeling that came over her was one that she would later describe as being hit by a car or jumping off something very high and landing in ice cold water. It knocked the breath from her lungs. It left her numb and light headed. She felt as if her heart stopped beating for a second, and maybe it had. There was something in the baby's eyes that reminded Jude of herself; that called out to her, desperate for her attention. She took one step forward, reached out to touch the child, before taking two steps back. It was nuts. She rejected the strange feeling, forcing it from her mind. Jude Mikhale had no children. She was young, irresponsible and broke, and more importantly, this Gideon guy was a dangerous lunatic. All of her energy was needed to figure out how to get away from him. After she was free, she would find out who that baby actually belonged to, and return it to its real parents who were no doubt worried sick.

It took some time for Jude to reach the conclusion that there were no "real parents"- worried sick or otherwise. There was DNA in that baby's veins that looked exactly like the DNA in hers. No, it didn't make sense. And yet...

Sleep came back to Jude slowly, but eventually it found her and she slept right through until morning. When she awoke, she found Shiloh lying quietly awake, running her fingers through the holes in a small knit quilt she called "blankey". The sun was shining behind the curtains, the storm long past.

"Morning," whispered Jude as she poked Shiloh in the ribs.

The little girl giggled and sat up. "Finally," she said, rolling her eyes. She crawled to the edge of the bed. "Let's get up!"

"Wait," said Jude, holding onto Shiloh's skinny arm. Her eyes hadn't even adjusted to the light yet, and her body was still heavy with sleep. The clock on her nightstand read 7:45 a.m. "I have a better idea. Let's lay here a while longer and just listen to the sounds of the morning. Maybe even fall back to sleep. That's what weekends were invented for." Despite how delightful it sounded to her, Shiloh looked back at her with deep skepticism.

"No," she said with conviction. "Weekends were invented for having fun!"

"And you don't think sleeping is fun?"

Shiloh shook her head.

"Trust me, you will." She looked at Shiloh with pleading eyes, but Shiloh was unphased. "Yeah, alright," answered Jude, defeated. "Let's get up."

After the coffee was gone, Shiloh ate a stack of waffles inside of a box that she had drawn windows on. She'd stuffed it with all the toys she could fit and was playing happily, so Jude sat down on the couch and began flipping through tv channels. She stopped on channel 9, a local news station, and saw that there had been some sort of incident in town. The screen showed a police car, blue lights flashing, parked in front of a home near the library. Jude turned up the volume.

"Police are still investigating a strange attack that occurred in Acadia City around nine o'clock last night," said a tall brunette news anchor. "Miss Elma Wood was out walking her dog Max on the wooded trails by Liberty Lake when someone- or something-jumped out ofthe bushes and attacked her."

The screen then showed an older woman, probably in her seventies, with bruises on her arms and a small scrape down her left cheek. "I don't know what it was," she said, obviously shaken. "I'd never seen anything like it before. When it knocked me down, I hit my head. I think I fainted, and when I woke up, Max was gone."

The woman began to sniffle and the screen cut back to the anchor. "Police found Max's leash a few yards away from the site of the attack. Max has not been recovered."

Someone off screen must have said something to the anchor. She smiled weakly with a nod, tapped a stack of papers in front of her with the bottom of her pen, and said, "Authorities believe there may be a black bear on the loose. It is recommended that all citizens avoid the lake area until further notice."

Then some news piece began about state wide burn bans and Jude turned off the television.

"Well, that's strange," said Ezra, peering over the stair railing.

"Yeah," answered Jude slowly.

"I didn't know bears came that far into town."

Jude hesitated. "No," she said, shaking her head. "Pretty sure they don't."

"You don't think it was a bear, do you?"

She looked back at Ezra with skepticism written on her face.

Jude stood up from the couch and knocked on the crayon-drawn cardboard door on Shiloh's box. "Anyone home?" Asked Jude.

Shiloh poked her head out. "Oh, yes, come in," she said. "You're just in time for tea."

Jude knelt down to be at eye level with the roughly cut cardboard window. "I'm sorry, I can't stay for tea today," she said. "I was just coming by to let you know that I need to make a phone call and will be in the kitchen."

"*Mom,*" said Shiloh in frustration. "You're not supposed to say stuff like that." She leaned into Jude's ear and whispered, "I'm playing a game."

Jude tried not to laugh. "Oh, of course, I'm sorry." Jude stood up. "Well then, I'm going to town for a little while. I'll be back."

"Okay," answered Shiloh with a smile. "Wait," she said. Her voice fell back to a whisper. "Town means the kitchen right?"

"Yeah," Jude whispered, then leaned down to kiss Shiloh quickly on the head.

Ezra followed her into the kitchen where Jude pulled out her cell phone. "It doesn't sound like a bear to me," she said, scrolling her contacts list to find Gideon.

Ezra took a seat at the table and her face darkened with worry. "I hope whatever it is, I didn't bring it to town with me."

Jude shook her head. "I doubt you did. This kind of thing is going to happen anywhere we go. It's hard to hide from an all-powerful evil..." Her voice trailed off and she put the phone to her ear.

Gideon answered after two rings.

"Hello, Jude, I was expecting your call. How are you? Has Ezra arrived yet?"

"I'm fine. Yeah, she's here. Thanks for the advanced notice, by the way," she said.

"Well, like I said in the voicemail, I only found out about it myself yesterday. So she is adjusting well?"

"Yes," answered Jude. "Everyone's fine. But listen, I have another problem. There's some story about a little old woman whose dog was eaten by something going around on the local news channel. The police are saying it was a bear. But I have a bad feeling about it."

"Well, that could mean something," Gideon confirmed. "It's important to trust your gut. But why couldn't it have been a bear?"

"Because the woman said she'd never seen anything like it before," replied Jude. "She was very shaken up. Don't you think if it were a bear, she would have recognized it? Also, black bears don't just attack unprovoked."

There was a pause on the other line.

"What do you think I should do? I should do something, right?" asked Jude.

"Well, it is definitely interesting. You may consider talking to the woman who was attacked. See if you can get a description from her."

"Yeah, I'll try that," answered Jude.

"Let me know what you find."

"I will. But-?"

"Yes?"

"If it's not a bear, what do we do? Do we move again?"

Gideon cleared his throat. He was probably sitting in his living room with a cup of coffee and a puzzle on the table in front of him. "Well, Jude," he began. "You could move again. You could spend your life on the move if you wish. But no matter where you go, you will find trouble. My advice would be that you eradicate it quickly and live as comfortably as you can. I'm here if you need me."

CHAPTER 3

"What's the plan?" asked Ezra eagerly, hands folded on the table in front of her.

Jude sat down across from her. "Gideon thinks I should go talk to the woman who was attacked. I just hope she's coherent enough to talk to me," answered Jude.

"Well, what about going to the police? Could you get the real story from them? I'm sure they asked her to describe the *bear.*"

Jude was shaking her head in disagreement before Ezra was even finished speaking. "We can't go to the police. If this thing wasn't a bear, they will not be able to imagine the alternatives we're interested in."

Ezra nodded. "I guess that makes sense."

Jude weighed her options. She had to speak with this woman. Although it was the middle of the day, she did not want to risk bringing Shiloh along, in case there was some horrible monster out there. But she wasn't ready to leave Shiloh alone with Ezra. Ezra certainly wasn't prepared to talk to Mrs. Wood herself and Jude wanted first hand information. She was going to have to give something up. Gideon said that Jude could trust Ezra. And she trusted Gideon with her life. So that had to account for something.

Jude paced through the room with her phone still in her hand.

"Okay, here's what we'll do," she said finally, stopping in her tracks. "All of us will go to this lady's house, Elma Wood, and you and Shiloh will stay in the car. I'll tell her I'm a reporter. Hopefully she believes me."

Ezra quickly agreed to the plan, and Jude pulled Shiloh out of her box-house without explaining very much of what was happening. She grabbed a notebook and a pen and headed to the Jeep.

Jude strapped Shiloh into her car-seat and they made their way down the driveway toward town.

"Do you know what you're going to say?" Ezra asked as they turned the car onto Main Street.

Jude thought for a moment. "I guess I'm just going to ask her what she saw." She looked down at her faded jeans and old NYU t-shirt. She was in such a hurry to get moving, she didn't think to change before they left the house. But then, she had no idea what reporters wear, so this was just as well. Miss wood was old, maybe her eyesight was bad.

They pulled up in front of a small, yellow house in a quiet neighborhood. "Looks like someone's home." Jude said quietly to Ezra, looking through the windshield at the car in the driveway. "I'm going to leave the keys in the ignition. If something should go wrong, which I don't think it will, I want you to take Shiloh and drive. Call me as soon as possible." Jude glanced back at Shiloh, smiled, and switched into an overly calm, reassuring voice. "I'll be right back, baby," she promised, then got out of the car.

She rang the doorbell, and waited for a few seconds until the door opened and a woman in her forties answered. Jude straightened her spine and tucked her spiral bound notebook under her arm. "Hello, my name is Jude Mikhale. I'm a reporter for the Daily Acadian."

Before she could go any further, the woman interjected. "Listen, I don't think my mother is feeling up to any more reporters today. I'm sorry."

"I understand," said Jude. "The police would just like to get a description published in the paper so that if anyone sees it, they can report it."

"She's already given a description to the police," said the woman. "Have a nice day." She began to shut the door.

"Wait," Jude stepped forward toward the door. "That description was off the record. I can't use it in the article. Please? You would be doing the community a huge service."

The woman sighed. She glanced back in the living room at her mother, and then back at Jude. "Fine," she said, opening the door all the way. "But this needs to be quick. She's not feeling well."

"Thank you so much," answered Jude. "I promise it will only take a minute."

Jude glanced back at the Jeep where Ezra was watching her out the window, then went inside. The house smelled like an old person, and was clean, but cluttered with little framed pictures and ceramic figurines on shelves and tables. On a small reclining chair sat a small, gray haired woman who easily blended in with the nick-knacks scattered around the house. She looked tired. Her face was slightly scraped, and down her cheek was a small line of stitches. She was in a nightgown and thick socks, sipping tea.

Jude made her way to the frail lady, and sat down on a loveseat near her. "Hello, Miss Wood," said Jude softly. "My name is Jude. I'm so sorry about all that's happened to you."

Miss Wood smiled softly. "Thank you, dear," she answered in a frail voice.

"Would you mind if I asked you a few questions about what you saw?"

Something in Miss Wood's eyes seemed to spark. She began speaking before Jude could ask any questions. "Yes, but you won't believe me," she said frankly. "None of them have. They all say it was a bear." Her voice was frustrated and sarcastic. "I told them I know what a bear looks like but the police looked at me like I was old and incompetent and just laughed. I swear, the nerve of some people these days. To think that I don't know what I saw."

Jude opened her notebook. "I believe you, Miss Wood," she said, ready to write. "I really do. So, you tell me, what did you see?"

Miss Wood sank back a little at the memory of the image. "It was large," she said. "Much taller than me. Not that that's saying much." She spoke evenly, like she wasn't really in shock at all. She was more surprised and confused than anything. Jude listened patiently.

"It was probably six feet high. Maybe more. It's skin was... strange. It wasn't covered in fur like a bear would be. It had skin, but the skin was discolored. Almost gray. Or green, like a sick person. And it was wrinkled and deformed. When it grabbed me, it felt cold."

"Mama," said the woman who let Jude in. "Are you sure you're not imagining all of this?"

Miss Wood looked at her daughter with angry eyes. "Sarah, don't treat me like a mental patient. I know what I saw! You're just as bad as the police." She looked back at Jude. "I didn't imagine it." She touched Jude's arm and Jude looked up from her notebook. "I didn't imagine it," she said again, intensely.

Jude nodded. "I really believe you didn't," she said. "What else did you see?"

Miss Wood released Jude's arm and put both of her hands together, fingers interlaced on her lap. "It had sharp teeth. It snapped my Max's leash right in half. I saw its eyes," she said quietly. "They were frightening. Kind of yellow, and like an animal. Like there was no one behind them." It seemed that at that moment, something occurred to her. She leaned in closer, glanced cautiously at her daughter before whispering to Jude. "I believe that all living things have a soul, even animals. Spend any time at all around my Max and you'll believe it too. But, I got a strange sense from that thing. Something I'd never felt before. It touched me and I knew that it didn't have a soul."

Sarah shook her head in frustration on the chair across from Jude. "This is ridiculous," she said. "You're encouraging her to believe this insanity."

Elma smacked one hand on the arm of the chair. "I'm not a child!" she yelled. "I do not need encouragement!"

The daughter stood up and left the room.

"It's okay," said Jude once she heard a door close down the hall. "It's hard for some people to understand these things. But I do."

Miss Wood looked relieved. She took a deep breath and calmed down. "You said your name was Jude, dear?"

"Yes ma'am."

"Well, Jude. I am telling you, as sure as I live, the *thing* that attacked me and my dog in the woods was neither a man, nor a bear. I've lived here my whole life and seen my fair share of black bears. This was unlike anything I've ever seen. If I didn't know better, I would say it wasn't of this world at all."

Jude gave a reassuring smile. "Thank you, Miss Wood. That's all I need."

As she stood up to leave, Jude felt Elma's hand on her arm again. Her eyes were a little wild as she whispered, "you're no reporter, are you dear?"

Jude grinned. She leaned down to Miss Wood's ear. "Let's just keep that between us, alright?"

Elma Wood nodded with a smile, and Jude walked back to her car.

When she opened the door and climbed into the driver seat, Shiloh was singing an old song with Ezra that Jude had never heard before.

"Ezra taught me a song!" Shiloh said cheerfully when Jude climbed in.

"It sounds beautiful," answered Jude. She quickly reached back, touched Shiloh's skinny leg, and buckled her seat belt.

"So, how'd it go?" Asked Ezra once Jude started the car.

“Went well,” said Jude, somewhat faltering. “It certainly wasn’t a bear,” Jude continued. “I think we may have something here.”

“What are you going to do?”

“Well,” Jude began. “Tonight I’ll go out, I’ll find it, then I’ll kill it.”

Shiloh looked up suddenly. “What’s going on, mama?”

“Nothin’ baby, don’t worry about it,” Jude answered, making a note to speak more quietly. She turned back to Ezra in a whisper. “Here’s the thing. Where there’s one, there’s usually more.”

CHAPTER 4

Once they were home, Shiloh begged Jude to let her play outside. Her favorite toy was a large wooden castle that Gideon had built for her. He spent months on it, sawing, gluing and painting. She had dozens of castle figurines that fit inside of it. She loved to bring it outside and play with it in the grass. Instead, Jude convinced her to play in the basement. Ezra followed Jude to the basement door, which opened to a wooden staircase. At the bottom, Jude flipped the switch, illuminating her in-home training arena.

"Woah," Ezra said quietly. "You have a whole gym in your basement."

This was no ordinary gym. There was ordinary work out equipment, of course. In one corner was a Total Gym contraption, where one piece of equipment served as multiple workout machines. There was a treadmill next to it. But beyond that, nothing was of the usual. Hanging from the ceiling were three punching bags of different sizes. There was a puffy foam target in the far back of the room, and around it were throwing knives, axes and a crossbow. There were training mats all over the floor, boxing equipment on a shelf, and a modest collection of old, medieval looking weaponry. There was a small shelf with a couple of old looking books, covered in dust, surrounded by several small bottles of holy water, and hand carved wooden crosses.

"Do you know how to use all of this?" asked Ezra.

Jude nodded. "I spent a lot of time training with Gideon. Almost four years. He's really into his deadly weapons."

"I've heard about him. Never met him though. Maxwell always spoke highly of him. He's the Synedrion guy who arranged for you to get Shiloh, right?"

"Yeah," answered Jude, casting her glance toward the corner to make sure Shiloh hadn't heard.

"Oh, I'm sorry," whispered Ezra, bringing her hand to rest on the side of her face. "I guess she doesn't know?"

As she wrapped her knuckles in tape, Jude quickly shook her head. "No, not yet. Anyway, we lived with Gideon until we moved here. He taught me a lot about fighting, though I wasn't completely unfamiliar with the concept before we met." She offered a sideways grin. "You think this is a gym, you should see the one in his basement."

"Why weren't you training while you were in college?"

Jude began to stretch and warm up her stiff muscles. "Because I had no idea there was anything to train for."

"You didn't know?"

Jude laughed. "No. Two weeks before I met Gideon I had lost my scholarship to NYU for dropping below a 2.5 GPA. I had no idea this was going to happen. If someone had tried to warn me I would have told them they were crazy."

"So then, how did they convince you to go with them?

Jude sat down on a weight lifting bench and continued to stretch. "Well they didn't. I had just dropped out of school that morning. I remember I was walking from my apartment to this bar I used to meet friends at and I started to feel really dizzy and sweaty. I was walking up the steps to my apartment when someone attacked me from behind, covered my mouth with a damp cloth, and I passed out. I woke up several hours later in Gideon's living room with two duffle bags stuffed with what they could grab of my things sitting next to me." She pulled her right arm across her chest and felt her shoulder loosening, pulling the muscles down the right side of her spine.

"They kidnapped you?" Ezra gasped. "That seems like a terrible plan."

Jude nodded. "It would have been a terrible plan if there was anyone to come looking for me, but they knew there wasn't. They started a weak rumor that I'd run away. About a year ago, I Googled myself to see if there was a missing person's report or anything. Nothing. I left New York and became a completely different person."

"You don't have any family at all?"

Jude shrugged. "Not that would be interested enough to hunt me down. I had been living with my aunt and uncle after my parents died, but I'm pretty sure they took the runaway story hook, line and sinker. I have a brother, Jimmy, someplace, but he really did run away, before I even left for NYU. I have no idea where he is. And when he knew me, my name wasn't Jude Mikhale. Mikhale is the name of some great grandmother, the bloodline name. Jimmy would look for me under my father's last name."

Ezra picked up a heavy sword and swung it around. "How did you not know?" asked Ezra. "I mean, I didn't know my whole story until I was like sixteen, but I always knew there was something going on. I knew that I was different."

"Well," Jude began, laying down on the bench. She put her hands around the cold iron of the dumbbell. "This gig wasn't exactly intended for me," she explained. "See, I had this cousin, Jacqueline. My mom's sister's kid. Daughter of the aunt and uncle I was living with. She was a few years older than me, and kind of a mystery. My parents just said her family was *confused*." She lifted the weight from the hooks and felt it's heaviness in her shoulders. "My mom said that her mom, my grandmother, used to tell stories about our family being special, and that her sister took it a little too seriously. I guess it was supposed to be her all along. But she was killed just before my parents, and like them, it wasn't exactly an accident. I was sixteen. My whole family had a target on it's back. Everything evil wanted us eliminated. With us gone, there would be no one to carry out the destiny. So the Synedrion had to find her replacement real fast and I was next in line. Gideon said that I had always had it in me, it was just laying dormant, waiting to be needed. But I was not who they expected. It took some tweaking of the plan to make this happen."

Ezra nodded along intently, and moved around the room, picking up weapons and testing them in her hands. She liked the way Jude talked. She had a fairly ungraceful way of speaking, direct and self-deprecating, with a low, controlled voice and dark sense of humor. Despite her walled-off persona and the way that her northern accent and terse vocabulary gave her a hard edge, there was no guarding the vulnerability in her tone. It was as if her words represented facts, but not entirely truths, always a little unsteady, and just on the other side of them, on the inside as each was being formed and delivered, was a person in deep contemplation, protective of those thoughts which were unsightly and sometimes unreasonable, but kept her mind always buzzing.

"That's wild," Ezra answered in amazement. "I can't even imagine. I guess your grandma was right, though." She lowered her voice and nodded in the direction of Shiloh. "So, she is yours though, right?"

My daughter? Oh, yeah, she's mine," Jude grunted, lifting the weight back up and returning it to it's holder. "The Synedrion kidnapped my DNA long before they kidnapped me. They extracted my blood, unbenounced to me at the time, when I was passed out in the hospital with a broken ankle. At the right time, they used it to create Shiloh. They came back for me the day she was born, and I met her three days later. Crazy to think that for a whole nine months, my kid existed, carried by some Synedrion woman I'll never know."

"Wow," Ezra mulled over the idea and finally gave an audible exhale. "I was trained by the Synedrion, too," she said after a minute's pause. "But not this much. They told me that I would better learn to fight when I met you."

"What did they teach you then?" asked Jude, as she set the weight back up on the hooks and glanced at Shiloh who was playing in the corner, setting up her castle.

"Well, I was so young at the time that they mostly just educated me. Math, science, history. That kind of thing. But my education was supplemented with classes about weird things. Demonology, Parapsychology, Biblical history, ancient civilizations and religions, mysticism, theories of magic. Stuff none of my friends at Lafayette High School were learning."

"I guess not," answered Jude.

I took a few semesters of Jujitsu, one of Tai Chi. But I didn't get to do much weapons training. What about you?" Ezra asked. "What were you studying at NYU?"

"If I tell you, you won't believe me," replied Jude. She had not mentioned her college life, or anything prior, to anyone since Shiloh.

Ezra laughed. "Try me."

Jude shook her head, but having already surrendered, she reached into the images that flooded her mind when she thought of her past. "I was a dancer," she answered with a slight grin. "I had an amazing artistic scholarship, and I was studying dance at one of America's most beloved schools." She almost didn't believe it herself, it was so long ago. She remembered the music, the theatre, the hours of back breaking exhaustion, the thrill of warm lights and a full auditorium. She couldn't have been more distant from that person now.

"Wow," Ezra said. "You're right, I don't believe you." She put the sword back on the stand and walked closer to Jude. "You seem a little... dark for dance."

Ezra feared she'd overstepped until Jude laughed and blinked up at her. "Why were your grades so bad? Did you just not like it?" she continued.

Jude widened her eyes. "I loved it. Dancing

was great. My mom got me into ballet when I was four, and I couldn't stop. It was everything else I sucked at. All my other classes suffered. Usually I didn't show up. Then dance started to suffer, too. I started not dealing with my problems. Filling holes with other things that weren't so good for me." Jude paused, and wondered why she was saying so much. Usually, she was not a long talker, but she had been lonelier than she realized. It was nice and refreshing to have someone to talk to; someone with whom she could be honest. "I guess I just felt out of place. Like I wasn't where I was supposed to be in life. I always felt like something was missing."

Ezra nodded. "Well," she said. "You were right."

Once the training began, it lasted well into the evening. Shiloh, as usual, was completely content sitting in the corner and playing, aside from the few times when she needed to go upstairs to get a drink, or a snack.

Ezra was competent, a little clumsy, but practice would eventually fix that problem. Jude was on fire. It had been a while since she got in any good training. Most of her time in the last few months was spent working out the logistics of the move, the story she would tell people, how she would handle life on her own. Not to mention that training alone was no fun. It felt good to get back into fight mode. It made her feel like she was getting somewhere. Like she was safe. Indestructible.

She kept thinking about the thing that attacked Elma Wood. She decided to throw all of her energy into reassuring herself that no matter how big or bad, she could kill it. With every blow to the punching bag, she pictured the creature hitting the floor. With every swing of her blade, the creature was in pieces. By the end of the day, she was wiped out. So was Ezra, whom Jude had thrown into the training mat dozens of times.

Jude made dinner for everyone with the supplies she had gotten from the market that morning. She wasn't much of a cook, but she and Ezra were so hungry it didn't matter, and Shiloh was happy with anything. At the table, Shiloh kept Ezra and Jude entertained with stories about her castle adventures, and the plans she had made for her future.

"I want to be a sailor when I grow up," she said in between bites of warm cinnamon apples.

Jude forced the corners of her mouth into a gentle smile. She had gotten the idea from an old poem that Jude read to her on many nights. Shiloh loved stories and poetry. Every night was a book or a poem. And Shiloh, though very young, grasped at any and all ideas that she could from them. The next day, her games would always incorporate the story from the night before.

Sweet, tiny Shiloh. It pained Jude to listen to

her ideas about the future.

"A sailor?" Jude asked, shoving her emotions back down where they belonged. "What will you do as a sailor?"

Shiloh shrugged casually. "I could catch whales," she proposed.

"What will you do with them when you catch them?" asked Ezra.

"Well, I'll take their picture and let them go."

Ezra nodded. "Maybe you should be a photographer. You could take pictures of all kinds of animals."

Shiloh seemed to like the idea. "Yeah, like dolphins and turtles!"

Jude ate the last bite on her plate and looked inquisitively at Shiloh. "But you would have to be on a boat way out in the ocean. Wouldn't that be scary?"

Shiloh shook her head. "No, it won't be scary. You will be with me."

The air in Jude's lungs evacuated in one short exhale. She stood from the table choking on hard gasps. She kissed Shiloh on the top of her head and hurried out of the room, forcing herself to maintain composure as she fled. For a few minutes she paced around, fighting off the impending panic attack, trying to put out of her mind the reality of Shiloh's existence, her calling, her death. Jude took deep breaths and attempted to regain focus by telling herself that she would find a way to prevent it. She would move heaven and earth if she had to. She would die if it came to it. Nothing would take Shiloh away. Finally, Ezra emerged from the kitchen behind her. Jude felt a hand on her back. "Are you alright?" Ezra asked.

Jude shook her head. "No," she said, refusing to turn around and face her friend. "She won't have a future, Ezra."

Ezra took a step closer as Jude closed her eyes tightly. "Jude," she whispered, looking for something of value to offer her.

Jude shook it off, unwilling to let herself slip any further in front of Ezra. She felt herself going weak and couldn't let that happen. "I need to get out there." She looked out the window at the sky, almost dark but glowing slightly from the recently arrested sun. "I need to find whatever monster attacked that old lady and kill it before it causes more damage."

Ezra tightened her shoulders and laced her fingers together in front of her, silently agreeing to drop it. "What are you going to do?"

Jude sat down on the couch and rested her head in her hands. She took a deep breath and exhaled slowly, still focused on Shiloh. "I guess I'm going hunting."

Shiloh came skipping into the living room and climbed into Jude's lap. Jude wrapped her arms around her and squeezed her until Shiloh let out a small cough. "You're squishing me!" she squealed.

Jude relaxed her grip and looked up at Ezra. "I can't bring her with me tonight," she said. "I guess I'm going to have to leave her here with you."

"I'll keep her safe. I promise."

Jude nodded and ran her hands through Shiloh's soft, sandy hair. "Ready for bed?"

Shiloh sighed but didn't fight as Jude scooped her up and carried her up the stairs. She playfully tossed her down onto her bed, then walked around the room, checking all the window locks.

"What are you doin', mommy?" asked Shiloh, brushing her messy hair from her eyes.

"Oh, nothing," answered Jude. "Let's get you into your pajamas."

Shiloh lifted her arms over her head and Jude pulled off her shirt. She wriggled out of her jeans and pulled on her favorite purple nightgown. After she was in her pajamas and tucked into bed, Jude pulled out their book of Shel Silverstein poetry and sat down on the edge of the mattress. Keeping up with their nightly ritual, Jude held the book out to Shiloh, spine down. Shiloh placed one hand over her eyes, and stuck out her other index finger. She placed it on the ridged pages, toward the middle, and Jude opened the book at that spot. There were four poems across the spread, and she read them all to Shiloh, who lay quietly listening. The poems were for children and most were silly. Shiloh would giggle quietly, and the giggling would turn to silent smiles, and when Jude finally got to the last poem, the little girl's eyes would start to flutter and close.

After the poems were read, Jude closed the book, kissed the top of Shiloh's sleepy head, and headed for the door.

"Goodnight, mama," whispered Shiloh, turning over to fall asleep.

"'Night baby," answered Jude. "Sweet dreams."

She left the door cracked open so the light from the hallway spilled in just a little, then went back downstairs to find Ezra.

She placed her hands on her hips and tried to steady her mind as the idea of leaving Shiloh alone with Ezra came back to her. "I need you to watch her like a hawk," she said, pacing and talking too quickly.

"I promise. I'm going to go upstairs and sit at my desk. I will be able to see her from across the hall."

"Okay," Jude answered. "I need to get some supplies. I'll be right back."

She disappeared into the basement and came back with a supply of weapons: a cross, a wooden stake, and a sharp silver dagger.

"I see we like the classics," stated Ezra.

"Gideon says if it's not broken, don't fix it."

Ezra laughed. "Fair enough."

Jude tucked the stake and dagger into a small purse that she carried over her shoulder, and placed the cross in her jean pocket. The sky was dark now, and Jude wanted to get an early start on the hunt.

"I'm not sure how long I will be," she said, moving for the door. "Send me a text message every thirty minutes, so I know everything is okay." Maybe she was being paranoid. She really didn't care. "She's a deep sleeper, but sometimes she gets up for water, or has a bad dream. Call me if anything like that happens and I'll come right home."

"I will," answered Ezra. "Don't worry. Just find the bad guy and get rid of him, okay? I'll hold down the fort here."

Jude nodded. "Lock the door behind me, then check the rest of the locks. Windows too."

Ezra smiled. "I will."

"She's everything that matters in the world, Ezra. Don't take your eyes off of her."

Jude stepped out of the house and shut the door behind her, then waited until she heard the lock click.

CHAPTER 5

She drove into town, to the small lake where the incident was reported to have happened. After parking the Jeep back from the road, she wandered into the woods, following the trails that snaked around the water.

The atmosphere was eerie. The night sky was heavy and deep, sprayed with a dusting of white stars that shimmered on the still, brown water. A thin fog rose up from the lake's surface, thickening the air and blurring the edges of her surroundings. The forest was dark, dense, and hollow, made up of tall poplars and oaks, visible only as towering silhouettes against the blue-black night. Every sound elevated Jude's heart rate. But it was always only the wind, or a racoon, or a deer. Nothing abnormal. Certainly nothing paranormal.

She made her way around the lake, stepping carefully along the rock-peppered dirt path. Once she had returned to her starting point with no success in finding the thing, Jude took to the sidewalk. There wasn't much on this particular street. There were a couple houses here and there. Television lights glowed from a few windows. Someone was arriving home and getting out of their car and waved as Jude walked past. No one seemed concerned for their safety.

Ezra's first text message came through as Jude stepped onto the blacktop.

"Hello! Everything is fine here. Shiloh is sound asleep. Hope you're onto the guy."

Jude responded to let Ezra know that everything was okay, and that she had no leads but was still looking.

As she continued to walk, she came to a cemetery in the yard of a church. It was old, but looked like it was still taking new residents. Jude could see the glow of freshly glossed marble in the moonlight, and piles of dirt off to the side indicated recent digging. She turned in and left the path, walking through damp grass and over graves. As she was walking, something caught her eye. One headstone looked particularly new. The ground around it was still raised, and in front of it were several flower arrangements. As she got closer, she pulled out her cellphone to use the flashlight. The headstone was definitely new. The man's name was Paul McCormick, and he died only a week before. Even more interesting, the ground appeared to have been disturbed, and one of the flower pots had been knocked over. There was dirt pushed up and tossed aside, and it looked like someone had been trying to cover it back over, because there were sweeps through the soft clay as if a hand brushed the area flat.

Jude bent down and discovered that the dirt was very loose and crumbling. In the cell phone glow, she could make out a hole a little more than a foot in diameter. She stuck her hand inside it and continued to lean in until her arm was fully extended. She had still not reached the bottom. There were scratches on the marble that almost looked intentional, like someone had taken a pen knife and etched a half-moon shape beside Paul McCormick's name, but amid all the disturbance around the grave, it was easy to assume the stone could have gotten scratched. She exhaled heavily and stood up, brushing the dirt from her hands. This was certainly a good indication of what may be lurking in the woods.

She looked around to make sure no one saw, then she swept the hole back over with her foot. When she was satisfied with the appearance, she sat down next to the headstone to think of a plan.

While the thought of some undead thing lurking around town made her uneasy, Jude was happy to have found the hole. At least now she knew that there was in fact something to be found. Miss Wood was not crazy at all. She knew, however, that where there is one, there has to be another because vampires don't just decide alone to be vampires. Something has to turn them from dead or dying humans to thoughtless reanimated monsters; to make them climb out of the grave after death. Jude wondered how long there had been vampires in this town. Was this a new development? Did this start when she moved in? Or was this some deep, dark secret that they had managed to keep quiet? Either way, it wasn't good.

It could be anywhere by now, but the sloppiness of the attack on Miss Wood indicated that it wasn't very *good* at being a vampire. The new ones never were. Sleepers, Gideon called them, were still in the state between deadly, manipulative fiend, and mindless, bumbling blood-hunter. It took weeks, even months, for sleepers to regain functionality enough to communicate and have the coordination to launch complex attacks. The troubling thing was, something much more adapted must have sired this one. It was probably still lurking close by, desperate for something – someone – to eat.

Jude developed a plan. If this sleeper wasn't too bright (and most of them were not) , then she could simply use herself as bait. She walked back to the lake slowly, hoping to lure it out of wherever it may be hiding. Once back, she took a seat on a bench near the woods line. It wouldn't be too willing to go far from the cover of the forest.

She had fought sleepers, and even stronger, full-fledged vampires before, more than once. It was a simple concept: throw a few punches, stake to the heart, from dust to dust. They were not rational creatures. They weren't feeling, thinking, or processing, but were more like brainwashed foot soldiers of the damned. Usually, they were regular people turned by some far more powerful demon promising ultimate freedom and immortality. Of course, they would never actually get to make good on these promises. When they came back from the dead, they were different. Animalistic. Single-minded. Completely under the control of their sire and primal urges. They wouldn't recognize the people they loved. They wouldn't remember who they were before.

Jude always won these fights. She could think and plan and be cunning and they could not. When it was over, Jude always felt that she had gained more skill, more strength, more speed from the experience. The more she fought, the more she grew into herself.

Another text message came in from Ezra. And another. And another. Time seemed to be crawling, and nothing was happening. Just as Jude was about to move to another spot, something caught her attention. Out of the corner of her eye, she spotted movement. The motion, though unclear, was accompanied by a sharp sound, like that of a branch snapping. She turned to the tree line, and saw the form more clearly behind the trees. It was hunched over, moving awkwardly around and headed her way. This had to be her guy.

Jude pretended not to notice, and turned back around, waiting for the sleeper to take the bait. She flipped through her phone messages as another update from Ezra came in. No change. All was well. She could hear the clunky footsteps getting louder; drawing nearer. Jude opened her purse and wrapped her fist around the wooden stake.

"Hello," snarled a slobbery voice from behind her. Mr. McCormick's undead voice, she presumed.

Jude turned to face him, doe-eyed, and smiled. "Hello," she replied. Her hand silently determined which end of the stake was sharpened. His face was deformed. His eyes and cheeks were sunken in, and his lips were ghostly pale. His complexion was a milky gray, and saliva dripped from the corners of his mouth. Most disturbingly, he reeked of death and rot.

"Are you here waiting for someone?" The monster growled.

His slurred speech and robotic movement indicated that he was not strong, but had been resurrected maybe a week before. He had likely been surviving on squirrels and other animals in the woods. Or someone was feeding him. "No," she answered. "Just came out here to enjoy the quiet."

Jude felt a pang of remorse for him. He may have been a handsome man. He was probably only in his forties, and still wearing his burial suit. She could see small rips and tares where he had clawed out of his grave and ran through briars, and she wondered why he died so young.

Then his mouth twisted into an ugly grin and his upper jaw began to quiver, revealing the sharp points of two fanged teeth. He was breathing heavily and his breath was warm and canine. With a grunt, he lurched forward to grab Jude by the arm, but before he could, she grabbed him by the collar of his suit with both hands and threw him off of her.

The sleeper went flying back about four or five feet. Jude stood and pulled the stake out of her purse. As she reached him, he was standing and dusting himself off, looking confused. He went in again for the attack, and Jude punched him in the stomach. Feeling little pain, he recovered and threw a punch at her, hitting her square in the mouth. Jude tasted the metallic twinge of blood on her tongue, but kept fighting. She, too, had a natural-born high pain tolerance.

Jude assumed he had not had much to eat since he was resurrected. His body was cold and lifeless, unlike the hot, veiny, surging bodies of monsters with a full belly. He leaned in to bite with every attack and his teeth snapped shut inches from her ears.

She knocked him off balance and thrust him to the ground. His shoulders squirmed and he struggled to release his arms but he could do nothing under her pin. Jude lifted the stake over his chest and was prepared to plunge it into his heart. As she looked down to her target, she noticed the glossy corner of a photograph peeking out of his breast pocket. With the stake gripped in her palm, she pulled the picture out with her two fingers. The faces of a happy family smiled back at her. A beautiful woman held the hands of two young boys, and behind her, smiling and proud, stood Mr. McCormick.

In a moment of human weakness, Jude lost the upper hand. He kicked one leg up hard, and she felt it hit her back, knocking the wind out of her. While she reacted to the pain, he grabbed her shoulders, threw her onto the grass beside him and dove on top of her.

Jude felt the grass beneath her back, cool and damp. His hands pressed into her shoulders. He was sitting on her stomach and she couldn't move or breathe. Her chest felt like it was going to collapse under the pressure.

She was already out of breath, and the struggle seemed useless. She flailed her forearms and tried to shove him off of her but he was not relenting. She could feel her heart rate accelerate and pound on the inside of her chest. She didn't feel strong. She felt afraid. Fear flooded into her brain as she thought desperately for a way out.

He said nothing, just looked down at her neck with protruding fangs. The stake was still in her hand and she turned her head to look at it, a useless stick in a useless hand.

He took a deep breath and dove in toward her. Her head was the only thing she had left, so she used it. She smashed her forehead into his and he flew back, gasping and coughing. She had stunned him and in that moment, she broke her right arm free. He was still sitting on her stomach and she lifted the stake and plunged it through his back, accessing his heart from behind. He looked into her eyes, moved his mouth to speak, and turned to dust on top of her.

Jude laid there for a moment catching her breath. When she determined that she was covered in dust she leapt up and brushed it off. She looked around the quiet park and out at the lake. Not a ripple on the water, not a breeze on the air. All was silent and still. Another message from Ezra had come in. She could feel her phone buzz. She didn't answer it. Slowly, she made her way back to the Jeep and drove home.

When she stepped in the front door, she found that she was moving slowly. Her back was sore, her lip, though the blood had dried, was throbbing, and her wrist seemed to have taken a lot of stress as well. She heard Ezra come down the stairs as she made her way into the living room.

"Oh, it's you," said Ezra, dropping the arrow of a crossbow to her side.

"Yep, it's me," said Jude weakly.

"Wow, you look rough," said Ezra, stepping closer. "Are you okay?"

Jude nodded. "I heal fast," she said casually, as she dropped down onto the couch.

Ezra disappeared into the kitchen and returned with a warm, wet washcloth and a glass of water. “Here,” she said, offering them both to Jude. “You need to clean up that cut on your lip. And the one on your forehead. And the one on your arm.”

Jude thanked her and took the towel and the water.

“So, what happened? Did you kill the guy?”

“Oh, I killed him,” she answered. “In fact, I probably still have a little bit of him on me.”

Ezra's eyes narrowed and her forehead wrinkled.

“Dust,” Jude clarified.

“Right. So, how was it? Was it just a vampire? Were there more?”

“It was just a vampire,” answered Jude, suddenly ashamed that something so simple did so much damage. “He was the only one, but I know that someone sired him. So there is at least one more thing out there. Something worse than a vampire.”

“Could you get anything out of him? Maybe who sired him?” Ezra asked, inspecting a cut across Jude’s bicep.

Jude shook her head and took a sip of water. “They’re generally not very chatty.”

Ezra nodded. “Well, now what?”

Jude glanced at the clock flashing below the

television screen. It was after one in the morning.

"Now we go to bed," she answered, moving slowly to stand up. "There's nothing more we can do tonight."

Ezra pulled Jude up from the couch and the two went their separate ways at the top of the stairs.

Shiloh's bed was glowing in the yellow din of her nightlight a few feet from Jude's own bed. Shiloh was sound asleep under the covers. Jude kissed her softly on the head and limped across the room to lay down.

When Jude woke up, light was shining through the open window – had she gone to bed without closing it? Shiloh was leaning over her, nudging her ribs.

"Pssst, wake up," Shiloh insisted. Jude's eyes blinked open and squinted in the sun, until the blurr faded and she focused in on Shiloh's face, a mere two inches from her own. "You've been asleep forever."

Jude glanced over to the clock on the table. It was after ten. She sat up feeling stiff and awkward. She lifted her arms to stretch and retracted them quickly with a painful wince.

"What's wrong?" asked Shiloh, her little hands resting over Jude's arm.

"Oh, it's nothing," answered Jude, rubbing the sore muscles. Last night's fight must have been more intense than she thought. "Come on, let's get you some breakfast."

"I've already had breakfast," said Shiloh, springing off the bed and taking Jude's hand as she stood slowly. "That girl Ezra made me toast with honey. It was good!"

Jude rubbed her eyes and followed Shiloh downstairs where Ezra was on the couch watching the morning news.

"Morning," she said, sipping coffee.

"Morning," answered Jude. "Sorry, I never sleep that late."

"You had a rough night, it's no big deal."

"Well, thanks for feeding Shiloh."

"Sure," answered Ezra, smiling. "There's more coffee in the kitchen."

Jude made herself a cup of coffee and drank it slowly, going over the previous night in her head. She remembered the photograph in his pocket, the guilt she felt, losing her focus. A rookie mistake. She was more than a little embarrassed. After the coffee was finished, she forced herself to change into workout clothes and head to the basement. She didn't want a fight like the one the night before to ever cause her so much trouble again. She pulled on baggy sweatpants and a black tank top and got to work in the gym with Ezra. With her castle already set up, Shiloh played again in the corner.

"So, last night you said there were more vampires?" asked Ezra, between punches on the bag.

Jude pulled a knife she had just thrown out of the chest of a dummy. "I'm not really sure," she admitted. "I should probably come up with some kind of patrolling routine. But with Shiloh, I don't like going out late at night. And I'm not really sure where to start."

Ezra nodded and took a few more hits on the punching bag. "We can work something out."

Jude stood in front of a full body mirror and scanned herself. Cuts and scrapes from the night before were now scabbed over and looked mean in the dim basement light. Her hair was falling out of the loose bun she'd thrown it into and it was brushing her eyes. She looked somewhat frightening. And somewhat frightened. She turned back from the mirror and towards Ezra. "Honestly," she said, picking up a handful of throwing knives. "This is just the beginning."

Over lunch, Shiloh came running into the kitchen with her half eaten peanut butter sandwich. "Mom!" She squealed. "Mom, I need to tell you something!"

"What's up?" asked Jude, picking Shiloh up and putting her on her lap.

"I need to go to school," said the child. She picked up a grape from Jude's plate and popped it into her mouth.

Jude was startled. "You what?"

Shiloh swallowed the grape and took another one. "I need to go to school."

"Why?" asked Jude.

Shiloh laughed. "Mom, everyone needs to go to school."

"Well, everyone needs an education," Jude corrected. "But sometimes that happens for different people in different ways."

Shiloh narrowed her eyes and rolled the grape around in her palm. "What do you mean?"

Jude looked at Ezra who tried but offered no relief. "I mean, some kids learn at home. Some kids learn different things, too. Like less math, more armed combat techniques."

Ezra laughed and then clapped her hand over her mouth. Shiloh looked back at Jude very confused. "Mom, I need to go to school," she said, shaking her head. "So I can learn to read and do fun stuff."

"What fun stuff?" asked Jude. "School isn't fun." She realized this was maybe not what you should be telling your four-year-old, but the idea of sending Shiloh to school was horrifying. And for her, it had always been true.

Shiloh got excited. "Like recess and lunch time and art class!"

Jude decided that Shiloh couldn't watch any more tv. It was giving her dangerous ideas.

"Well, Shiloh, I'm really glad you want to go to school," Jude said earnestly, taking Shiloh by the hands. "But I'm not so sure that now is the right time for you to go to school. Don't you think we should wait until you are a little bigger?"

Shiloh fervently shook her head. "No, I think I need to go to school now."

Jude nodded. She placed Shilohs feet back on the ground and handed her a bunch of grapes. "Well, we will see," said Jude calmly, though her heart was racing. She stood up from the table and put her plate in the sink. "Go play some more and we can talk about it later, okay?"

Shiloh, who was satisfied with that response, ran back into the living room to play in her cardboard playhouse. Jude shot a concerned glance to Ezra before sitting back down and speaking softly. "How have I not thought of school?" she scalded herself, pressing her fingers into the center of her forehead. Eventually Shiloh would have to get an education. At almost four years old, she should be in preschool. She was a smart kid. Too smart, perhaps, and Jude knew that it wouldn't be long before Shiloh figured out the truth; that she wasn't like other kids. "I don't know what to do."

"Maybe you should call Gideon?" asked Ezra.

"Yes," said Jude, standing up again with cautious optimism. She picked up the phone. "Gideon. Good idea. Maybe he can convince Shiloh to wait a little longer."

Jude began pacing around the kitchen as the phone rang. After three rings, Gideon answered the phone.

"Hel-"

"Shiloh wants to go to school," Jude blurted out before Gideon could finish answering.

"Jude?"

"Of course! Who else would it be? Did you hear me? Shiloh wants to go to school! I don't know how she even thought of it. It's those damn tv shows she watches. There will be no more of that."

Gideon laughed softly. "Calm down. It's going to be fine, we can–"

"Gideon, do you understand what this means? How the hell am I supposed to protect her if I'm not with her?" She collapsed back into the chair and perched the phone on her shoulder, pinned up against the side of her head so that she could use her hands to rub at the growing ache at the back of her neck.

Ezra watched Jude unravel with her head resting on her fist at the table.

Jude heard Gideon adjust the phone. "Jude, listen to me," he said, calmly. "I understand your concern, but you are overreacting." Gideon had a naturally slow and easy voice that brought calm with it. "I can see that you have not thought of this, but I have. The child needs to go to school. She deserves that chance, don't you think?"

"Of course I do, but-"

"Good. The semester starts next month right? In mid-September?"

"I have no idea when preschool starts, Gideon," she retorted.

He laughed. "Okay, well I'm pretty certain it begins next month. That gives you plenty of time. Find a church school. One that is actually in a church. She will be safe there, at least for a few years. She should be around other children. It will be good for her. And you. It will give you the time to find a part-time job, or have some time to yourself to process things and to train. It will ultimately make you a better protector for Shiloh. You will be more focused."

"You're telling me to send her to school?"

"I'm giving you my opinion."

Jude exhaled. "Thanks for nothing."

"It will be okay," Gideon assured her.

She stuck her head into the living room and called for Shiloh. "Hey, do you want to talk to Gideon?"

Shiloh came bolting out of her playhouse. "Paps!" she yelled, accepting the phone from Jude's hand. Shiloh had taken to calling him Paps just before they left Indiana. She had no idea where it came from, but Shiloh had never really called him anything before that. He wasn't her grandfather, but the term of endearment seemed to bring Gideon some joy. Shiloh ran with the phone back to her playhouse and Jude listened to her giggle from outside the cardboard wall.

CHAPTER 6

September came too quickly, and by it's arrival, Jude and Ezra had worked out a pretty effective schedule. The increased paranormal activity in Acadia demanded that someone be constantly on the lookout. Jude went patrolling every other night, while Ezra stayed home with a usually sleeping Shiloh. On the days between patrols, Jude and Shiloh would go into town and Jude would try to stay apprised of the goings-on, or any talk of strange incidents.

Townies seemed mostly unaware of any change. Things had settled since the incident with Miss Elma's dog and, though Jude was convinced that most people knew something was up, they continued to deny it. Ignorance is bliss, and so they wanted to remain as ignorant as possible. Jude would run into some nasty, fangy evil about once or twice a week, which seemed like a lot for a town where nothing ever happened. But she couldn't get any of them to talk, and they all turned to dust when she plunged a wooden stake through their heart. All vampires. Low on the hierarchical scale, and paid in blood to do the bidding of bigger, badder things. Which meant that bigger, badder things were out there somewhere.

Shiloh, of course, had no knowledge of Jude's

patrolling, or of anything abnormal. Jude routinely wrestled with the idea of when to tell her, and the only conclusion she could ever draw was *later, when she's older*.

She turned four on September 1st, a Wednesday, and the celebration was small, but warm. Jude baked a cake and decorated the living room with purple ribbons and balloons. Gideon sent her a book about dragons and Shiloh loved it. She ate her purple cake and blew out her five purple candles (one for good luck) and ran around in a sugar high until she fell asleep into deep purple dreams.

Shiloh wouldn't stop talking about school. She even started practicing her letters and numbers so that she could be ready when class started. The day after her birthday, Jude took her to St. Mary's, the only Catholic church in town. Conveniently, it was also home to St. Mary's Early Learning Academy. She hated the idea of private school, with their pretentious names and preppy soccer moms, but, there was a giant brass cross affixed to the front door of the church, so it would do.

Jude wrapped her hand around the giant cross and pulled open the heavy wooden doors leading into the church. On the other side was a vestibule with red carpet and dark wood walls. There were several lamps scattered around on various tables, each emitting a yellowish glow, illuminating the room only a little. On a waist high table there was a stack of service programmes. A cork board on the wall advertised several church meetings and activities. With Shiloh tagging along beside her, Jude opened another set of doors and stepped into a large sanctuary. The red carpet continued into this room, and so did the dark wooden walls. The ceiling was vaulted, and intricate chandeliers hung from exposed squared beams. There were rows of pews covered in red upholstery, and lining the walls were colorful stained glass windows depicting images of Christ, the Virgin Mary, and various Bible stories Jude recognized from childhood. It was a breathtaking room with a quiet, sacred atmosphere. At the front of all the pews, the floor took two steps up, and turned into a pulpit and stage area, where there was a beautiful pipe organ, an altar, and a stack of books and readings on a small table.

Shiloh walked through the rows of pews and ran her hand over the velvety cushions. She casually strolled up to the front and stopped at the altar. Her fingers played across the engraved word *Sanctus* carved into the wood.

"Shiloh, I'm not sure we are in the right place. Come on," said Jude, preparing to leave the sanctuary.

Shiloh sat down on the floor before the altar and stared up at the pipe organ, and the large depiction of the Crucifixion above it.

Jude sailed toward her, equally intrigued and creeped out by this place. "Come on, kiddo. We need to find the school. Let's go –"

As she reached for Shiloh's hand, a man appeared from a door behind the organ that Jude had not noticed before.

"Holy," he said loudly in the thick silence of the sanctuary. He seemed to be watching Shiloh admire the wooden altar. Jude couldn't see him very well in the dim light.

"Excuse me?" asked Jude, gripping Shiloh by the arm.

"Sanctus," he clarified, shifting some papers under his arm and clearing his throat. "It means *holy*. It's Latin."

"Oh," answered Jude, pulling Shiloh to her feet. "That's good to know. Come on, Shi." She began pulling the girl toward the front door.

"I didn't mean to startle you," said the man. You are welcome to stay. Can I help you with something?" he asked.

"Um," Jude stammered. "Actually, we're looking for St. Mary's Academy. Is it in this building?"

"Oh," answered the man. He took two steps toward them and into the light of a chandelier. "I can help you with that. It's in this building, you just came in the wrong entrance."

Jude was stricken with the recognition of Christopher, the man from the market several weeks back. "Great," she said as she gave him the once over.

He was dressed professionally, like the first time she'd seen him, in black slacks, a white button up and a dark grey sportcoat. His face was sharp and angular, and he had the makings of a dark five o'clock shadow lining his jaw up to his freshly cut, slightly disheveled chestnut hair. His staggering green eyes met hers advisedly, and he offered a very faint smile. Once again, though, the intensity of his gaze alarmed her. She didn't fear him, but wasn't sure she trusted him. There was something unspoken between them.

"If you'd like, I can take you there. Just let me swing by my office and drop these things off." he nodded to the stack of papers in his hands.

"Sure, thank you," Jude answered.

She followed him back through the door he had come through, and down a maze of old hallways and narrow doors. He moved quickly and with a wide gate leaving Jude, and especially Shiloh, struggling to keep up.

"You're Jude, right?" he asked without looking at her, as they made their way down a marble tiled hallway.

Jude hesitated. "I am," she said. "We met at the market."

He stopped suddenly at a door with a brass name plate that read, "Christopher Alighieri."

He shuffled into the room and left the door

open behind him. “Right,” he said, with his back to her. “I tried to rescue you from Doris. I hope I wasn’t too late.”

Jude could see into the office. The desk was messy and piled high with books and papers. He had things tacked to the walls, not in any order. He set the papers in his hand on top of more papers on the desk and shuffled some things around. He was a blur, constantly moving, shifting, fidgeting. In the movement, he uncovered a book that caught Jude’s eye. *Exorcism: The History of a Controversy.*

Just as quickly as he went into the room, he came out. Jude offered a polite laugh. “No, you came just in time,” she replied, her mind still on the book on his desk.

“Oh, good,” he said. He ran a hand through his hair, which left it even more messy. “Sorry about the pit stop. It’s been a long week for me. Things are piling up.” He motioned for Jude to continue following him down the hall. “Uh, so,” he said. “Are you looking into sending your daughter to school here at St. Mary's?” He glanced at Shiloh and smiled.

“Yeah,” answered Jude. “Do you know anything about it?”

“Well,” he answered. “We have a small student body, plenty of adults to keep watch, and the teachers are all really creative and involved.”

“That’s great,” said Jude, walking beside him.

"Are you a teacher?"

"Oh, no," said Christopher. "I'm an assistant to the priest. It's just an apprenticeship while I work on my masters."

Jude nodded. "I see."

"Here we are," he said, opening a set of double doors into what was clearly a preschool. There were large pin boards on the walls covered with coloring pages and student work, and across from where they stood was a glass-walled library decorated for the new school year.

"Woah," said Shiloh quietly. "This looks like fun!"

As she stepped toward the colorful artwork, mouth open and eyes wide, Jude knew Shiloh was not going to take no for an answer. She was going to school.

He led them to another office door and looked at Jude. "So," he said abruptly. "This is our stop: the Headmaster's office. He's a really nice guy and I'm sure he can answer any of your questions."

"Thanks a lot," said Jude.

He nodded. "This is a safe place, I assure you."

Jude hesitated to respond. Something in the way he'd said *safe* – it reminded her again of the odd feeling of familiarity between the two. She wanted to know what he knew. Chances are, he knew nothing and was just offering friendly assurance to an obviously worried parent. That's what she told herself. "I'm sorry we interrupted you," she said, choosing to let it go one more time.

He shook his head. "Oh, no, I'm glad you did. I needed a break." He smiled. "Well, good luck and if you need anything in the future, you know where to find me. It was nice to see you again, Jude."

He spoke her name in a way that caused the pit of her stomach to flutter, just a little, then he looked at Shiloh. "Have fun in school," he said. He offered her a smile and she returned it and waved goodbye as he turned to leave.

CHAPTER 7

Shiloh, being Shiloh, was not afraid to start school at all. She understood very well that she would only be away from home for a few hours, and that her mother would always come for her. So when Jude walked her into her classroom on the first day, Shiloh barely listened as Jude spoke to her.

Jude had prepared for this moment, and brought along something special, in a small gold box.

"Shiloh," she said, kneeling down next to her. "I have something for you. It's very important, okay?"

Shiloh looked all around her at the other kids playing in the classroom.

"Shiloh, are you listening?"

"Oh, yeah, I'm listening," she said, glancing for only a moment at Jude before her eyes darted away again, eager to take in the scene before her.

"Shiloh, look." Jude opened the gold box and showed Shiloh the cross necklace that was inside.

Shiloh became somewhat more focused and touched the cross with her index finger. "Pretty," she said smiling.

"It has your name on it." Jude pointed to the

tiny letters imprinted on the pendant.

"Oh," said Shiloh, once again becoming distracted by the commotion around her.

Jude removed the necklace from the box, put it around Shiloh's neck, then took both of Shiloh's hands in hers. "Listen to me baby," she said softly. "Don't take this off, okay? Not for any reason. It will keep you safe."

"Ok, mama, I won't," Shiloh promised. "Safe from what?"

"Just, anything. It will keep you safe from everything."

"Okay," answered Shiloh. "Can I go play now?"

Jude looked in the direction of Shiloh's gaze where some kids were playing with finger paint and wearing stained aprons. She sighed quietly, so Shiloh wouldn't hear. "Yeah, you can go. You sure you're okay?"

"I'm fine!" Shiloh answered. She threw her arms around Jude. "I love you!" Then she turned into the classroom and joined the kids at the art table.

Jude had to take a moment. This may not have been difficult for Shiloh, but it was difficult for her. Watching Shiloh walk away and into that classroom felt like a swift punch to the gut. She was nervous and emotional and hesitant to leave. Not because she worried that something terrible would happen at school. Because Shiloh was her baby, and she was growing up.

The teacher glanced at Jude and gave her a sad, understanding smile. Jude stood up and laughed it off. She watched Shiloh playing with the other kids for just a moment. When Shiloh noticed her mother still standing by the door, she smiled and waved. Jude waved back, then turned to go home.

As she made her way out of the building, she met Christopher on the front steps as he was coming in.

"Oh, hi," he smiled. He seemed more collected than he had on their previous encounters. "This must be your daughter's first day. Shiloh, right?"

"Yeah, it is." Jude answered, pressing her index finger into the corner of her eye to deter one brave tear from springing loose.

"Not handling it well?" He asked with a laugh.

"Ugh, I'm trying. Had to peel myself away from the door, but I think I'm making progress."

"Oh, trust me. I've seen a lot worse. Red faces, tear streaks, running mascara. Some moms just don't leave. And when the dads come, they're even worse."

Jude laughed and crossed her arms in the cooling breeze. "Well, then I guess I'm doing pretty good."

"I think so." A brief silence fell between them, and he looked at her intently. Almost like he'd lost his train of thought but was still somewhere with her. After just a few seconds, he broke his glance and looked down at the steps, then back up at her more casually. "Well, I hope Shiloh is happy here. She seems like a good kid."

"The best," said Jude with confidence. "I think she will be. She's desperate to go to school."

"Well, that's a good sign." He shot her a quick smile, then he tipped his head toward her like he was about to walk away, but Jude was suddenly in need of a distraction, and decidedly determined to figure out what it was about him that struck a chord with her. Why did he look at her like he had known her for a long time? Like he knew some secret about her?

"So you're in school?" she asked, not completely tactfully.

"I'm finishing my master's online. A few days a month I drive out to the Seminary in Richmond to participate in activities and group meetings, but mostly I'm here."

"Seminary? So you're studying religion?"

"Divinity," he clarified. "I have a Bachelor's in Religious Studies."

Jude nodded. "So, you're going to be a priest?"

He shrugged. "More or less. I could be, if I wanted to be."

"Interesting," Jude lied. Being a priest was

about the most boring profession she could think of. "Why?"

He looked at his feet and back at her. "I want to help people," he said earnestly." And I thought it would be a lot easier if I had the Big Man on my side." He grinned.

When Jude looked puzzled, he laughed and pointed upward. "You know, the Big Man."

"Ahh," she said. "Well good luck."

He crossed his arms. "Thanks. And what do you do?"

Jude was taken off guard. She had no intentions of being on the receiving end of questions. "Uh," she stuttered. "Well, I'm kind of between jobs."

"What jobs are you between?" He had a smirk on his face, and she decided that she preferred him in his disheveled, nervous state. How had he gotten the upper hand?

"Well, if you must know, I used to be a dancer." She spat out the only thing she could think of. Then she recoiled, already regretting it.

"Used to be? Why used to be?"

She could feel sweat beads building at her hairline. "Well, I have a four year old. I'm hardly in the shape I used to be in." This, of course, was a complete lie. She was in the best shape of her life.

"That's not what it looks like to me." His cock-eyed smile struck her as uncharacteristically bold. She couldn't tell if he was flirting with her, or just being polite.

She swallowed the lump in her throat. "Oh yeah?"

He laughed, and buried his left hand in the pocket of his pants. With his right, he touched her arm, just below her shoulder, and held it there for a moment, like he was learning something about her through the physical contact. He dipped his head just slightly towards hers. "I hope we run into each other again. It's always a pleasure."

"Yeah," she answered. "I'm sure we will."

He turned to go inside and she watched him for a moment feeling dazed and confused, then continued down the steps to her car. Another weird encounter which left her a little dizzy, and no closer to understanding the guy she couldn't stop running into.

When she got home, she found Ezra sitting on the couch in the living room. She looked like she'd just woken up. Her hair was tangled, she wore glasses where she usually wore contacts, and her knees were pulled up to her chest and tucked into her bulky sweatshirt. She held a cup of coffee between her two hands, with all 10 fingers wrapped around the warm mug.

"There you are," she said when Jude walked in. "I was beginning to think you refused to go inside and Shiloh had to drag you."

Jude rolled her eyes. "It went just fine. The kid is happily playing with finger paint and I didn't sob or beg her not to go in or anything. But it's been an interesting morning," answered Jude.

Ezra raised her eyes. "Tell me more."

Jude turned toward the kitchen to grab a cup of coffee. "Meet me on the front porch," she said.

Jude got her coffee and joined Ezra outside. There were few things about the house that Jude didn't like. It's size had taken her some time to get used to, and for a while, she was concerned that it could be haunted, but for the most part, she really loved it. Of all the things she appreciated about the house, the porch ranked at the top of the list. It was wide and spacious, covered by a red tin awning, like the rest of the roof. The sun hit it just right in the afternoons, and it made the perfect place to sit with a book, or morning coffee, or even just to think. A porch swing hung on one side of the door, and there she sat next to Ezra. The early sun was still climbing over the mountains and the air was crisp, and smelled of cut hay and the beginnings of fall.

"So, there's this guy," Jude started.

"Oh no," answered Ezra, surprised.

"No, it's not what you think," answered Jude. "But he's kind of weird. He does this staring thing."

Ezra scrunched up her forehead.

"Not in a creepy way," Jude said quickly. "Or maybe it is in a creepy way, I don't know."

She told Ezra about their first meeting at the market, and his working at Shiloh's school, and their encounter that morning. Ezra sat cross legged on the porch swing and listened intently.

"So do you like him?" Ezra asked after the story was finished. "It sure sounds like he's got it for you."

Jude quickly looked away. "That is not the point of this conversation, Ezra," she defended. "And besides, I don't know," she said, pretending to pay a great deal of attention to a small hole in her jeans.

Ezra laughed. "You're smiling," she said. "You like him."

Jude laughed a little and took a sip of her coffee. "No, I mean," she adjusted in her seat. "He's nice and polite and freakishly good looking," she hesitated. "But I'm really in no position to be dating. Plus, I'm not sure he likes me like that. There's something up with him."

"Up with him?"

Jude picked at the denim tare. "You know, like

maybe he's evil."

Ezra laughed. "He's a priest."

"Not yet he isn't. And that doesn't mean he isn't evil. I dunno, something is strange. I feel like he knows who I am."

Ezra leaned back in her seat and looked out over the field. "Well, maybe he does, although I'd say the chances are extremely rare. He probably just thinks you're hot."

"Oh, I'm sure," Jude said with a quick laugh. "Wait 'til he gets a good look at the enormous apocalyptic baggage I'm carrying. Trust me, it's a mood killer."

Ezra nodded her head in understanding. "You don't think it will ever be a possibility?"

"To be in a relationship with someone who doesn't know the truth? No, I don't think so."

Ezra nodded. "I dated a guy once who was an outsider. It was fun for a while but destined to fail. Got way too complicated."

"Have you ever been with someone who wasn't on the outside?" asked Jude.

Ezra looked into her nearly empty coffee cup. "Yeah," she said. "Once. His name was Adam. I was actually with him right up until I was sent here."

"What happened?"

"I broke up with him," she answered, flatly. "He knew about everything except you and Shiloh. I wasn't allowed to say anything about it, so I just left."

"Did you love him?" asked Jude.

"Yeah, I did," she answered.

Jude didn't respond.

"What about you?" asked Ezra.

"What about me?"

"Well, don't you have some sad love story? Someone who might still be wondering where you went? A guy you were with in New York before destiny called and you picked up the phone?"

Jude looked past Ezra at the blue-green mountains and thought for a moment. Her last months of college had been spent mostly alone, save for a few one-night encounters that were never meant to be extended into something real. "I had an angsty high-school crush my Sophomore year, but that ended when my parents died and I moved to a different school. I dated a little in college, but the bulk of my romantic encounters at NYU involved a lot of gin and I barely remember them." They shared a laugh. "But," Jude shook her head. "If you were to put everyone I've ever loved in a room... let's just say you wouldn't need many chairs. There's pretty much just Shiloh. So you'd need one chair. A really small one."

Ezra laughed again and leaned back on the

swing, looking out over the mountains. "Well," she said finally. "I still think you should keep this Christopher guy around. Maybe you could be friends."

"Maybe."

CHAPTER 8

It was October, and Shiloh had been in school for about a month. At first, it was strange not having her around in the day. For four years, Jude had spent all of her time with Shiloh, nearly every waking moment. Since Ezra moved in, she had been going out on patrols when Shiloh was asleep, but that was the most time they had spent apart. Most of the hours that crept by while Shiloh was at school, Jude spent wandering around the house. She would talk to Ezra, straighten up, and sometimes go into town for something or another, but without Shiloh's laughter and little voice filling the house, Jude was not herself. In the alone time, she found that she had come to define herself in terms of Shiloh. If Shiloh was happy, she was happy. If Shiloh was scared, she was bold to drive away the child's fear. Now, without a frame of reference for her own emotions in the afternoon, Jude pretty much waited around for the clock to say it was two, so she could go get Shiloh and be herself again.

It got a little easier as the days went on. Jude and Ezra continued to get to know each other, and Jude liked spending time with her. She was easy to talk to, and she very quickly became the best friend that Jude had ever really had. Ezra could talk about anything, and Jude remembered what it was like to have a real conversation that wasn't about the fate of the world. She hadn't had that in years. She had abandoned so much of herself when she met Gideon. Maybe that explained her dependency to Shiloh. Talking to Ezra gave Jude the opportunity to remember who she was as an individual.

Ezra was the granddaughter of Rev. Magnus Durand, who rose to fame among religious groups around New Orleans when he cast out a demon called upon by a Voodoo priest. As it turns out, Magnus Durand was a descendant of a powerful sect of cenobitic monks dating back to the 4th century A.D. It was this sect of monks who served as prophets, preparing the way for the first sacrificial child to enter the world. The same monks hand picked Jude's maternal ancestry to protect and guard it. Really, their two families, though worlds apart, had been joined together by an intimate secret thousands of years before.

Jude was settling into a routine. She was learning to use the time in the afternoons without her daughter to get things done, that way she could focus her attention on Shiloh when she came home from school. Then, every other night, after Shiloh was asleep, Jude would make her rounds through town. She had a route that she usually followed. She drove to town, parked at the farmers market, strolled up main street, cut through Liberty Lake Park, and made her way to Longwood Cemetery where she had encountered her first Acadia vampire. Then she circled back to her car and went home. On most nights she was only out for about three hours.

Shiloh was loving every bit of school. She came home every day with drawings or playdough creations and stories about her friends. Jude was happy that she was talking to other kids her age. Shiloh had a lot coming to her, and having friends around to keep her grounded in some semblance of normalcy could only help.

One Friday in October, while Shiloh was off at school, Jude had made herself a sandwich and was sitting on the couch flipping through the TV channels when she saw a picture on the screen of a little girl with feathery blonde hair and the word "MISSING" below.

She turned the volume up as a young newscaster tapped a stack of papers on the desk in front of her. "Acadia area parents are frantic today as the search for four year old Lacey McKinney continues. Police say the girl disappeared from her own backyard around ten o'clock this morning."

Ezra made her way to the bottom of the stairs. "What's going on?" she asked.

"A little girl is missing," answered Jude, unable to pull her eyes away from the screen.

"One eyewitness says that she noticed an unfamiliar car make several circles through the neighborhood around the same time, but never thought anything of it," continued the anchor. "The vehicle in question is a black Ford Explorer with tinted windows. At this time there are no other leads and police are still investigating. If you have any information that may help find Lacey McKinney, please contact the Acadia Police Department immediately."

Ezra looked at Jude. "I hope they find her. I can't imagine..." Her voice trailed off.

"This Lacey girl is the same age as Shiloh. Even looks a little like her." Jude stared at the picture of the skinny, blue-eyed child.

"Could just be an extremely odd coincidence," suggested Ezra.

Jude nodded. "It could be."

Ezra moved to the couch. "What are you thinking?"

Jude shrugged, still watching the news broadcast. "I don't know. It seems strange. I'm probably overreacting. I guess we'll just have to wait and see. We will give the police some time to sort it out on their own. Maybe more of the story will develop."

"Do demons drive cars?" Ezra asked, puzzled.

"I don't know," Jude answered quietly.

Jude couldn't settle it in her mind. She couldn't shake this girl's resemblance to Shiloh, and it ate at her. Something in her gut sensed a connection and it made her nauseous.

As the day went on, Jude continued to check back in with the news, and grew more anxious as nothing changed. Lacey's father made a brief appearance and begged for information, with bloodshot eyes and a trembling voice, and Jude's heart broke for him. As much as she tried not to, she couldn't help but imagine herself standing up there, instead of him. Sobbing in front of cameras and countless viewers. Desperate for scraps of info about her missing daughter. He was so helpless, wringing his hands as he choked on his own words. Jude didn't like feeling helpless. She was the kind of person to take matters into her own hands. But this man was clearly broken, and Jude wondered what would happen when that day came for her.

After Jude picked Shiloh up from school, the two of them spent some time on the front porch. The leaves were beginning to change as the air grew colder, and the mountain ridges encircling the house had taken on a fiery appearance, with splashes of red, gold and orange. What was left of summer had been quickly extinguished on a breeze that arrived early in the month, and it was almost officially sweater season -- Jude's personal favorite. Shiloh was content after a long day at school to sit snuggled against Jude's side and flip through a stack of picture books as Jude read one of Ezra's mystery novels and it was nice to watch the day fade into evening, to take a hiatus from worrying about all of the threats breathing constantly down their necks. With Shiloh safe at home, right next to her, Jude felt a little guilty but couldn't stop from feeling grateful that Shiloh was not Lacey McKinney.

That night, after a very informal dinner of mac-n-cheese and chicken nuggets in the living room, all three went to bed. It was not a patrol night, and for some reason, Jude was extremely tired. She had been struggling to keep her eyes open through dinner. She fell asleep soon after hitting the pillow.

At some point in the night, Jude awoke to the sound of someone calling her name. At first, she thought it was Shiloh, but when she looked, Shiloh was sound asleep. She then remembered that Ezra was asleep in the room across the hall. Quickly, she got up from her bed and went to see. She burst through Ezra's bedroom door to find that she, too, was sleeping. Jude stood there for a moment wondering if her mind had simply been playing tricks on her. She shook it off and went back to bed.

Before she could fall asleep, however, she heard the voice again. It wasn't loud, but seemed to be coming from every direction. It sounded as if it needed help. Shiloh hadn't heard it, and was still motionless, asleep in her bed. Jude got up once more and went to the window, this time more unsettled. It wasn't in her head, someone was calling for her. There was a light glowing outside in the yard. When Jude looked closer, she saw that the light was a lantern, in the hands of a dirty little girl in a white gown. The little girl had long blonde hair and looked familiar. After a moment of thought, Jude was struck with the realization that she had seen the girl before; it was Lacey, the missing girl from the news. Frantically, she ran downstairs and out the door where the little girl had been walking. When she got to the front porch, Jude didn't see her anywhere.

"Lacey," she called. "Where are you? It's okay, I'm going to help you." But she saw nothing. "Lacey, you have to come here. I can protect you. I can take you home to your parents." Nothing. Suddenly, Jude heard a crash, like glass breaking. She ran around to the back of the house to find a shattered lantern on the back sidewalk. In her haste, she hadn't thought to put shoes on and felt the stinging of glass shards under her feet. Fear was rising in her chest. She should have brought a weapon. What was she thinking? But she was strong and knew very well how to fight with her hands. "Lacey, where are you?" she called again into the dark. "Everything is going to be okay."

From behind a tree, a little girl appeared. "Jude, you have to help me," she whispered.

"Don't worry," Jude answered. "That's why I'm here."

The girl came closer, and Jude realized that it was not the same girl, not Lacey. This girl was in a blue dress, and her hair was still light blonde, but shorter. She was around the same age.

"Who are you?" Jude asked the girl when she was close enough to touch. "Where's Lacey?"

The little girl looked down at her feet. "I'm Samantha. Lacey is gone," she answered.

Jude knelt down and put her hands on the little girl's shoulders. "Okay, where did she go? I can help you both," she said trying to remain calm. The night was eerily still and quiet, and she squinted to make out the girl's figure in the pressing darkness. The stinging on the bottom of her foot grew worse and she lifted it off the pavement. Blood trickled out from two small cuts and she quickly tried to brush the glass away. "Samantha, sweetie, where is Lacey?"

"I'm not supposed to tell," Samantha whispered into Jude's ear.

At that moment, there was a loud bang and a scream from inside the house. Samantha grinned. "You'd better go," she said coyly.

Shiloh. Jude ran back inside and up the stairs, flipping light switches as she went. "Shiloh, I'm coming!" she yelled. "It's okay, I'm on my way!"

She flew through her bedroom door to find Shiloh gone and the curtains blowing in the breeze. "Shiloh!" she yelled into the night. "Shiloh, where are you?" Jude fell to her knees by Shiloh's bed, hands frantically shifting pillows and blankets, falling forever into an empty mattress. She grabbed at her chest where it felt like her lungs were collapsing. She didn't know what to do. Why was she falling apart like this? She was trained to fight. While looking down, she felt a hand on her shoulder.

"There, there, darling," sneered a cold voice. "You know you can't save them all."

Jude turned and looked to see a horrific being standing above her. It had glowing yellow eyes and a forked tongue. When it smiled, it's lips cracked and bled.

Jude stood to her feet, her strength suddenly returning and threw the thing down onto the floor. "What have you done with my daughter?" she yelled. "Where is she? I'll kill you!"

The being laughed. "I don't have your daughter. I have no reason to harm little Shiloh," it said. Its voice came from every direction. As it spoke, it's mouth did not move, but instead held a bloody, villainous smile. "I'm simply a messenger. Nothing more."

"You know where she is!" Jude persisted. "Tell me or you won't see the morning!"

The being laughed again. "You can't kill me, Jude. I would be gone before you could take a swing. Besides, I'm not your enemy. I'm your future." Its voice was cold and breathy, but steady. Not urgent in any way.

"What does that mean?" asked Jude, standing above the creature with her arms raised. "I'm nothing like you. You're a monster. Where is Shiloh?"

The creature shook its head. "I'm neither good nor evil. And I did not take your daughter."

"Then who are you?"

"You don't recognize me?" The thing spoke calmly with it's arms raised slightly. It's rotting flesh was blotchy and wrinkled. Thick, black liquid oozed from it's mouth where teeth were missing. It was a disgusting, deeply disturbing sight, but held itself like a person, upright. "I'm everything you are fighting against, but you can't kill me. You'll never beat me. I am inevitable."

Jude fell on top of the creature and began beating it.

The thing laughed and sneered and the room began to shake. Lights began to flicker as Jude yelled again for Shiloh.

"You can't harm me, Jude," the voice said as Jude's strength began to fail her. "I am death. Nothing more. You can't defeat me. I'm not a thing you can fight."

"No!" Jude shouted, her voice breaking and full of pain. "Where's Shiloh? What have you done with my daughter?"

An unseen force shoved Jude off of the creature and against Shiloh's bed. As she sat there, her back against the metal frame, bleeding and soaked from tears and sweat, everything grew still. The room was dark and quiet. Jude heard the footsteps of the creature drawing nearer but she was too weak to respond.

Jude blinked, only for an instant, and when her eyes reopened, there was the creature, centimeters from Jude's face. Close enough to smell the pungent, metallic odor of blood and saliva heavy on it's warm, damp breath.

"Please," Jude begged weakly. "Just give me my daughter back. Please don't hurt her."

The creature grinned. It reached out with its rough, scaly hand and stroked the side of Jude's face. "Shhh," it whispered. "Be still." At that moment Jude's vision blurred. She had been lulled into complacency. She felt herself sitting on the floor, watching, too tired to lift an arm. Too drained to speak.

The villain stepped back and nodded at Jude's broken body. "Until next time, my child," it whispered.

Something flashed. There may have been noise. Whatever happened, in an instant, it was gone.

Jude shot up from her bed, her heart racing and gasping for air. For a moment, she couldn't think.

She couldn't breathe. She felt as if something was crushing her chest, compressing her ribs and gripping her lungs. Looking around the room, she saw that all was normal. The lights were off. The windows were closed. Shiloh's sea turtle night light was glowing in the corner. Jude jumped out of bed and ran across the room. She collapsed beside Shiloh's bed and ran her hands over the covers. Shiloh was tucked safely inside, her breath slow and peaceful. It was just a dream. Just another, far more horrifying nightmare.

The bedroom door opened and light from the hallway fell into the room. "Is everything okay?" Ezra asked, stepping inside. "I heard some noise."

Jude exhaled and rested her head on Shiloh's bed. She closed her eyes and tried to slow the spinning. "Yeah, everything's fine," she said finally. "It was just a bad dream. Thanks, Ezra."

Ezra nodded then closed the door and went back to her room. Jude stood up, then bent over and scooped Shiloh up off of her bed. Shiloh's eyes opened for a moment.

"What's going on?" she asked, half asleep as Jude carried her limp, sleepy child across the room.

"It's okay," whispered Jude. "It's just me, go back to sleep."

It didn't take long; she was out again before Jude even made it back to her bed. She laid Shiloh down on a pillow, covered her with her big down comforter and climbed in beside her. With Shiloh there, sound asleep, Jude was able to rest. She closed her eyes, whispered a quiet prayer to God, whom she wasn't sure she even believed in, and drifted back to sleep.

In the morning, Shiloh slept late. Jude opened her eyes and rubbed them with the palms of her hands, still reeling from the nightmare. Careful not to wake Shiloh, she sat up and threw her legs over the edge of the bed. As the soft skin of her right foot fell on the cool, wooden floor, a sharp sting sparked from her heel and shot through her toes, and she involuntarily lifted it. As she rubbed the pads of her fingers over the cut, she felt the sharp edge of glass sticking out of her heel. A bitter cold chill rocketed up her spine and she found herself racked with a sudden rush of hot nausea, and calling into question everything she thought she understood about reality. Biting her lip and trying not to wince from the sting, she extracted the glass sliver and inspected it in the sunlight. It was a real, solid piece of glass. *What the hell happened last night?* Shaking it off, she got up, pulled on a big, heavy hooded sweatshirt and walked downstairs where Ezra was already up drinking coffee.

"Morning," she said cheerfully as Jude drug herself into the kitchen.

"Morning," Jude replied.

"There's more coffee in the pot," said Ezra. "You look like you had a rough night."

Jude nodded and poured herself a cup. "Mhm," she mumbled, acutely aware of the cut on her foot where the glass had been.

She sat down in a chair across from Ezra, and they looked at each other in silence for a moment. "So, what was your dream about?" Ezra asked.

Jude hesitated. Was it a dream? When she had woken up, the images were still so fresh on her mind, so tangible, that they seemed real. Now, she wasn't sure she'd ever gone to sleep. She considered calling Gideon. When she was living with him, he always asked her about her dreams. He said that sometimes they meant something, though often they didn't. He said it was crucial to be able to know the important ones from the unimportant ones. But, if she called him, he would definitely think this was an important one. He would want to come to Acadia and go out on patrol for demons and things that go bump in the night. Jude wasn't convinced that there was anything to find.

She shrugged. "I don't really remember," she lied.

When Shiloh woke up, Jude made her breakfast and they both dressed for the day. Shiloh asked to play outside, but after the missing girl from the day before, Jude was wary of the idea. Instead, she set Shiloh's play castle up in the basement, and she and Ezra trained for most of the afternoon.

Thoughts from her nightmare kept ringing in her head. *You'll never kill me.* It was horrifying, but something about it seemed genuine. She channeled all of her fears into her workout, digging deeper and deeper until she was wiped out and she had managed to shove the images from the nightmare deep out of her mind.

Around dinner time, when everyone was cooled off and cleaned up, Jude called to order a pizza. They all sat on the couch and ate while flipping through channels. Shiloh had the remote. She passed by the local news station in a hurry.

"Hey, hold on one second, baby, I want to see the news for a minute," said Jude.

Shiloh stopped surfing and the same anchor that Jude had seen the day before was on the air. She was just finishing up a story about some organization hosting a dog show fundraiser.

"To enter your k9 companion in the show, contact Margaret Adams for more information." The number came up on the screen, and the anchor flipped over a sheet of paper in front of her. "Tonight the police are still searching for four-year-old Lacey McKinney. Now, authorities say, another child has gone missing in Acadia."

Shiloh was holding a glass of grape juice and spilled it down the front of her shirt when she stood up. "Mama, look, I spilled my drink," she said.

"Okay," said Jude, placing a hand on Shiloh's shoulder. "Just sit tight for one minute."

She turned the volume up on the television. "Four-year-old girl Samantha Green disappeared from Washington Park this evening-"

"You have got to be kidding me," Jude mumbled, raising her hand slowly to rest against her lips.

"What's wrong?" asked Ezra. "Do you know her?"

Jude shook her head. "No, no I don't know her."

"Police are still investigating, and have reason to believe that these two incidents are somehow linked. If anyone has any information regarding the disappearance of Lacey or Samantha, please contact the Acadia Police Department right away."

The screen changed to a picture of the two missing girls. They looked like school photos. Both four years old. Both brunette. One in a white dress, and one, Samantha, in a blue dress.

Jude stood up quickly, pale with disbelief. Shiloh pulled at her shirt. "Mama, I need some more juice," she said.

“Alright, Shiloh,” Jude snapped impatiently. She picked her up and carried her into the kitchen with Ezra in tow. “Ezra, would you mind keeping an eye on her for a minute? I have to make a phone call,” asked Jude after pouring Shiloh a new glass of grape juice.

“No, I don’t mind,” replied Ezra. “Is everything alright?”

“I’m not sure. I’ll be right back,” Jude replied. “Just keep Shiloh in here.”

Jude left Ezra and Shiloh in the kitchen and stepped into the living room. She pulled her cell-phone out of her pocket and called Gideon.

“Hello,” he answered after only two rings. “It’s been awhile since you’ve called.”

“Hey,” Jude said quickly. “I need to talk to you.”

Gideon failed to sense Jude’s urgency. “Okay,” he answered calmly. “What’s going on?”

Jude spoke rapidly, the concern rising with her voice. “Listen, Gideon, I think something might be happening.”

Jude peeked into the kitchen and saw that Ezra and Shiloh were chatting at the kitchen table. She moved back into the living room and dropped her voice to just above a whisper. “Okay, yesterday on the news I saw a broadcast about a little girl going missing. I thought it was odd because she was Shiloh's age, and had similar features. And last night, I had this dream."

"A dream?" Gideon asked, his interest piquing.

"Yeah," answered Jude. "It was freaky, and in it I saw another little girl. Her name was Samantha. Today in the news, there's another little girl, also Shiloh's age, gone missing. Guess what her name is."

Gideon was quiet for a moment. "That's interesting," he said finally. "Other than the missing children, have you noticed anything wrong?"

"Nothing," answered Jude. "But Gideon," her voice narrowed. "This *was* the girl from my dream. I mean, they're identical. I saw her."

"Yes," he said quietly. "I can understand why you're concerned."

"So, what do you think? Does this mean something?" She switched the phone to the other side of her head and leaned against the wall.

"Well, it certainly is alarming," Gideon responded. "Prophetic dreams are not to be overlooked. I would suggest that you go out tonight. Spend some time in town. Do a little recon."

"I was planning on going out anyway. But I swear there's nothing to find. This is a weird little town you've sent me to. The people who live here, they're not normal. They know something's up, but they have no idea anything's up. You know?"

"People have a way of denying things that they can't explain. You should know."

"Whatever," Jude rolled her eyes. "I'm just saying that there's nothing to find. I don't know where to start."

"Oh, I guarantee that's not true," answered Gideon evenly. "Every town in the world has something of a dark underside, even Acadia. Small and quaint as it may be. You will know what to look for, Jude. Remember your training. You know how to spot something out of place. Stick to what you know and don't doubt your judgement. Start with the living."

They spoke for a few more moments and then said their goodbyes and Jude made her way back into the kitchen. As she walked in, Shiloh was right in the middle of a very serious and detailed description of her toy castle. Her hands were in the air as she talked about the tower, and Jude stepped up behind her and grabbed them. Shiloh jerked her head around and laughed.

"It's a pretty cool castle," said Jude to Ezra, still holding Shiloh's hands above her head.

Ezra looked inquisitively at Jude, but didn't say anything. Jude lifted Shiloh from her seat and noticed the grape juice stain down the front of her shirt. "Come on, let's get you in your pj's and ready for bed," she said. She looked at Ezra. "I'll be back in just a minute."

Jude carried Shiloh upstairs and finagled the child out of her clothes. Shiloh was unusually restless and reluctant to go to bed. She didn't want to be upstairs alone. It took two bedtime stories just to get her to lay down. A third to get her to close her eyes. Finally, after Jude sat next to her and rubbed her back for a while, she began to drift off to sleep. Jude tucked her in, and turned off the light.

"Sorry that took so long," she told Ezra, who had moved into the living room. "Shiloh is a little anxious. I'm not sure why. I know she's only four but I swear she can sense when something's up."

"She probably can," answered Ezra. "So, is everything okay?"

Jude sat down next to her on the couch and explained her dream, and the glass in her foot that morning. She told her that she had called Gideon and that he suggested she go into town.

"What do you think this is?" asked Ezra.

"I'm really not sure," said Jude. "It could be just some twisted sicko who gets his rocks off kidnapping little girls. Even if it isn't something supernatural, I have to do something. Two little kids are missing. It's sort of my job."

"What if it is something supernatural?"

Jude grabbed a wooden stake off the table and

crossed her arms over her chest. "Then I won't feel as bad when I kill it."

CHAPTER 9

Jude packed a backpack with a water bottle, flashlight and various weapons. She pulled her cross necklace out from under her shirt and left it dangling over her chest. Before leaving, she swept over the house. All the windows were shut, all the doors locked. She checked on Shiloh, sound asleep and safe in her bed. *As long as she doesn't wake up while I'm gone,* Jude thought. Shiloh would not react well to her not being there to comfort her.

Ezra waited downstairs by the door, with the phone in her hand. "Call me if anything happens. Anything at all. And keep an eye on the news."

Ezra nodded.

Jude threw her backpack over her shoulder. "Lock this door behind me, okay?" she asked, even though Ezra already knew the drill.

"Be careful," answered Ezra.

Jude stepped outside, waited until she heard the click of the lock, and stepped off the porch.

It was just beginning to get dark. The sun had set, but some light still lingered low in the sky. It was that in-between time where the moon was out, but the sky was still luminous, streaked with shimmering gold and rosy crimson, and the blue that remained was melting into a deep navy. Jude was exhausted, and hadn't even noticed until now, as she started the Jeep. She rubbed her eyes and rolled down the window to let the cool air sharpen her focus, then drove toward town, unsure of exactly where she was headed. This mission required a slight change in the usual route.

The streets were quiet for the most part. Occasionally someone would pass by walking along the sidewalk. All of the shops were dark, with *Closed* signs hanging on the doors. As Jude turned the corner onto Main Street, she saw a crowd of people gathered in someone's front yard, all holding votive candles. She pulled the Jeep into the parking lot of the farmers market, and made her way across the street to the house.

There was a couple standing on the front porch, looking over a sizable crowd of townsfolk. Jude determined that they were the parents of the missing girls. The woman was in tears, and the man had his arm tightly around her waist, as they spoke with faltering voices.

"Lacey is such a sweet girl. She is friends with Sammy, who also always has a smile on her face. We can't understand why anyone would do a thing like this. We are asking everyone to please stay on alert, as we will need all the help we can get to get these little girls back safely."

As soon as he finished the last sentence, the father's face erupted into tears. Someone from the crowd rushed up to hug both parents, while the rest of the group began to chatter.

"Tragedy," whispered the man next to her remorsefully, as he handed her a candle.

Jude nodded in agreement. Without glancing at the voice, she scanned the crowd. When her eyes met those of Christopher Alighieri, she stopped scanning.

He saw her and made his way through the gathering, nodding, shaking hands, and offering comfort to those he passed. When he reached her, he tipped the flame of his candle over the paper wick of hers and it sparked to life. "It's nice of you to come out," he said, one hand in the pocket of his khaki slacks. He looked different, more casual. His blue button up was untucked. No tie, no sportcoat. His face was slightly stubbled, like he missed a shave, and he wasn't carrying an armload of papers. In the fluttering glow of candlelight he seemed more boyish, more exposed.

"Well, I want to help if I can," answered Jude.

He faced away from the porch, toward the market. "You know, nothing like this really happens here," he began. "It's such a small town. You were probably hoping to get away from all the violence and drama. Now I bet you're itching to get away from here, too."

Jude watched her candle flicker. "Nah," she answered quietly. "No place is perfect. Even small towns have dark secrets." She remembered Gideon.

"Dark secrets?" he asked with quiet, doubtful laughter. "I've lived here for almost a year now and the only secret I've uncovered is that Miss Houser's famous peach cobbler comes from a box."

Jude grinned. "Maybe," she replied. He started to shift, like he was ready to move on, but she was not going to let him get away this time. "So, you've only lived here for a year?"

He leaned up against the front fence. "Yeah, I moved here to work at St. Mary's."

"Where did you live before?" Jude asked.

"Well, I'm from Maine, but I lived in Richmond for a long time."

"So," Jude continued. "You left Richmond, while in school, to come to this tiny, inconsequential town and study under a priest whose church has about seventy people in attendance?" She didn't even try to hide her suspicion.

Christopher hesitated and his eyes narrowed in on Jude's conspicuous gaze. "I go where I'm called, that's all," he said with a forced steadiness in his tone.

Jude took a deep breath. Wax began to drip down the candle. "Where you're called?"

"Well, where I feel compelled to go. Where I think I'm being led."

"By God?" Jude asked, trying to conceal her skepticism.

Christopher nodded, letting out a quiet laugh. "Yeah. Sounds hoaky, I know, but I believe I'm here for a reason."

"Okay," Jude responded. "What reason?"

Christopher shifted. He looked at her, then down at the ground. "Um, I don't know yet," he said finally. But she felt like he wasn't being completely honest.

"Well, you're new to town," she answered. "You seem to show up a lot. You are at every event. You pay close attention."

Christopher seemed surprised. "What are you suggesting, Jude? You're new to town, too. You're everywhere I am. Should I be looking at you as a suspect in the disappearance of these kids?"

Jude rolled her eyes. "Christopher, come on. Why did you move here?"

He ran a hand through his hair and twisted the candle between his fingers. "It's complicated," he began, suddenly evading Jude's glance. "You're going to think I'm crazy."

"Try me," answered Jude.

He gave a nervous look around, then grabbed Jude by the hand and led her across the street, into the market parking lot.

"Christopher, what the hell-" Jude started.

"Okay." He seemed belabored, like he was not looking forward to answering the question. "When I was in college, I had a dream."

"A dream?" Jude asked, already on alert. She'd had enough dreams, as of late.

"See, I told you it would sound crazy."

"It doesn't. Really. Please, go on." Jude crossed her arms over her chest and let the candle wax drip onto the pavement.

He sighed. "So I had a dream. But I wasn't asleep. It was the middle of the day. Kind of like a vision." He held her gaze for a moment to make sure she was still with him. Satisfied, he continued. "In the dream, I was in a small town, working at a church. A man in the sanctuary told me there was something I was supposed to do there. A calling. He didn't say what it was but the dream felt so real."

Watching him speak, Jude could feel the faith and confusion in his voice.

"When I came out of it," he went on, "I couldn't shake the feeling. For the entire day after, I was in a fog. Walking around outside of myself. I remembered the church I was working at in the dream was called St Mary's and started Googling. There are hundreds of St Mary's churches, but I did an image search and found the one I saw. It was this one. Exactly the same."

"Interesting," she said.

"So, I contacted the priest and asked if he would take me on as an apprentice. When he said yes, I knew I had to take it, so I left Richmond and moved here."

He looked back up at Jude with cautious eyes.

Jude pressed her fingers into the center of her forehead. "But you don't really know why you're here?"

He shrugged, hands in his pockets. "Nope."

A man with an empty cardboard box approached them and gave a quick nod to Jude before turning to Christopher. "Chris, we're out of candles."

"Oh, there are more in the van. I'll get them."

The man smiled appreciatively then walked away.

"Did you organize this?" Jude asked as Christopher shuffled around on the sidewalk.

He shrugged. "No, not just me. We thought we should do something."

"That's nice of you," Jude said earnestly.

"Oh, it's the least we could do."

They were silent a moment, listening to the chatter around them as the final embers of the day cooled into the dark wash of night. Someone was walking through the crowd, handing out flyers with the missing girl's pictures on them. Jude took one and studied their faces. They were beyond a shadow of a doubt the girls she had seen in the nightmare. She was unable to pull her eyes away from theirs on the page, full and bright, reaching out to her. Her mind leapt to Shiloh, asleep at home. What was she thinking? Someone–something–was going around looking for children to snatch and she left hers vulnerable. She pulled her cell phone from her pocket.

"Where's Shiloh at tonight?" Christopher asked suddenly, reading her mind.

Jude began to dial. "Um, she's at home with a friend. I'm just gonna call and check on her. Excuse me."

She stepped away into the street and hit send. By the third ring, Jude was hyperventilating. "Where are you, Ezra," she said aloud, pacing back and forth. Finally, after five rings, Ezra answered.

"Hello?" she asked.

Jude exhaled. "Ezra," she said, closing her eyes to steady her racing heart. "I was just calling to check on things. How's Shiloh?"

"Oh, she's fine," answered Ezra calmly. "Still sound asleep. It's been uneventful here. How about you? Have you found anything?"

"Not yet. There's a vigil going on in town. I'm going to try and talk to some people. See if they know anything."

"Sounds good," answered Ezra. "Don't worry. Everything's fine here. I'm sure you will find something."

"Thanks," answered Jude. "I'm gonna get back."

She hung up the phone and stood catching her breath for a moment. Before she made it back to the lot, Christopher was meeting her in the street. "Everything okay?" he asked.

"Oh, yeah," answered Jude as casually as possible.

He nodded slowly. "So, are you going to stay for a while?"

"Oh, no, I can't," answered Jude. "I have to get back to Shiloh. I just wanted to come out and see if I could figure- I mean, see if I could help out somehow."

"Gotcha."

"Yea," Jude mumbled awkwardly, her mind in another place. "Hey, so, do you know anything about these girls?" she asked, immediately reconsidering her phrasing. "I mean, the news isn't saying much. Did anyone see anything? Are there any leads on the attacker?"

Christopher looked quizzically at Jude. "Leads? Not that I am aware of," he said slowly, holding her gaze.

"Oh, ok," she answered, stiffening.

"If you're worried, I'm sure your daughter will be fine. These girls were taken from their homes right in town. You live at the old Wesley place, right?"

Jude nodded.

"Well, that's far enough out of town that I don't think you'll be bothered."

"Yeah, thanks," she answered. "I guess you're right. That helps a little."

His eyes narrowed and he stared at her. "Is there another reason you're asking?"

"Another reason like what?" Jude answered, and regretted it immediately. A simple *no* would've been so much better.

Christopher shook his head. "I don't know, but it seems to me that-"

Jude whipped out her phone even though it had not gone off. "Shoot," she said. "I've got to take this." She made sure to hold the screen out of his eyesight. "It was good talking to you, Christopher," she said as she turned to walk away.

"Yeah, but Jude, I-" She heard him call behind her, but she pressed her silent phone to her ear, pretended to talk, and hurried off into the evening.

Before heading to her car, Jude walked through town. It was nearing nine o'clock, and the dark autumn sky was spattered with stars. Jude did not want to return home with nothing.

As she strolled along the empty sidewalks, a breeze of relieving cool air swept between the buildings. Jude walked past the library, which may have been a good source of information, but it was closed, as were all of the shops on Bridge Street, with the exception of a bar called Henley's. She figured that, maybe, inside were some town gossips who would be willing to spare some ideas about the disappearance of Sam and Lacey.

Jude pulled open the glass door and stepped inside of a smokey, dark room. It smelled like alcohol, cigarettes and cheap bar food. It was not all that crowded, but there were a few people sitting at the long bar, and a table or two taken. Jude walked confidently up to the bar and placed both hands on the counter, receiving a few curious looks.

The bartender, a man in his fifties, drug a towel across the counter and asked her what she wanted. She hadn't really had a drink since college, save for the occasional glass of wine she'd had with

Gideon, but in the old days, she could really knock a few back. She hesitated before ordering a rum and coke, and asked the bartender to go easy on the rum. She handed him her ID and he turned to make the drink.

At the bar were mostly men. They glanced over at her a few times but were more focused on some football game on tv. She'd hope that her presence there would pique their interest. It did not. She even tried her patented flirtatious hair flip at a few strategically timed intervals but nothing. Apparently her ability to flirt had been discarded along with other now useless information she'd picked up in college. She was a little disappointed. The bartender handed her her drink, and she took a sip. The rum warmed the back of her throat in a very familiar way, and she let it sink in. If she was going to talk to these guys, she was going to need to go to them. She looked at the television screen and gathered that they were watching a college game between Auburn and Alabama. She had no opinion on football. Or sports at all, but she could pretend. She waited for a few minutes, until Alabama scored a goal. When they did, two of the three men cheered, and so she cheered too. This got their attention.

"You here for the game too, miss?" asked one of the men. He was older, probably sixty. He was a big guy, with suspenders holding up his pants and a red and white baseball cap with the Alabama elephant mascot on it on top of his grey-haired head.

Jude shrugged casually. "Just stopping in for a drink."

"Well, you've picked the right team. Why don't you come sit down here and join us?"

The old man was unthreatening, and the other two men, who were about his age, were looking curiously at her. She moved down two bar stools to sit next to them.

"I'm Eddie Bennett," The man said. "These are my buddies, Hank Carlson and Willie Clyde."

"Jude Mikhale," she answered, accepting a handshake. The other men said hello and went back to their game.

"From around here, Jude?" asked Eddie. Jude shook her head and took another sip of her drink. "Nope. From New York," she said. "But don't judge me too harshly." She shot him a sweet smile and he laughed.

"Well heck girl, I'm from Boston. Been here an awful long time though, twenty eight years."

Alabama scored another touchdown and Eddie and Hank cheered. Eddie leaned down the bar at Willie and said, "Looks like the next round is on you, buddy."

Willie rolled his eyes and called over the bartender.

"How long you been here? Don't believe I've seen you around," Eddie inquired.

"Oh, not long, actually." Answered Jude. "Just a few months. But I like it."

'Yeah, it's not a bad place to be."

Jude saw her opening. She took a sip of her drink. "It's not," she said. "But I was surprised to hear about those little girls. I figured this for a pretty safe little town."

Eddie looked down at his glass and shook his head solemnly. "It's a damn shame," he said. "The first girl Lacey, she's my cousin's son's girl. Sweet little thing, too. I hope they find her, and the bastard that took her. Around here, he'd be safer in jail. Lord knows if I happen to be the one to catch him, he's not gonna make it to a fair trial."

While Jude listened, Hank and Willie had started to listen in as well. When Eddie finished, Hank spoke up. "I don't know, Ed," he said casually. "I don't think he's from the area."

"Why not?" asked Jude.

Hank shrugged. "Well, everybody knows everybody here, ya know? Everyone's up in everyone else's business. If we had a creep like that hanging' around, somebody would know for sure. But everyone is accounted for."

"I think it was a gang," said Willie.

Hank and Eddie laughed. "We ain't got no gangs here you old drunk," said Hank, slapping Willie on the back.

Willie got visibly frustrated. He smashed his fist onto the bar. "I think we do," he insisted. "Things have been gettin' weird around here lately. First that thing with Elma's dog. Come on, that was no bear. And people have been talkin', you know. Maybe if you'd get your head out of your ass you'd hear it, Hank."

Hank rolled his eyes and grumbled under his breath. Jude laughed quietly. "Alright, well what have people been saying?" asked Jude. "Why do they think it's a gang?"

Willie shifted in his seat and dropped his voice low. "Now, I don't want you to think I'm some kind of crackpot, but people have been seein' things. I talked to a couple guys at the golf course just yesterday who said that they had seen some kind of punky, shadowy guy skulking around in their yards. They said he was dressed real funny, and was wearin' a mask or something. Both saw the same guy. And you know what? They both live in the same neighborhood as Lacey and Samantha."

Jude nodded. "That's strange," she said, taking another sip. The slowly melting ice was making the drink weaker and weaker, taking the sweetness away from the soda and leaving only the hot, mollassesy twinge of rum.

"Yea, it is, and you know what else is strange?" said Willie, leaning over the bar closer to Jude.

"Oh no, here we go with the conspiracy theories," said Hank.

"You shut up," Willie said loudly. He looked back at Jude. "These gangsters have some kind of symbol they were wearin'. Krantz told me on the golf course. He said the guy he'd seen in his yard was wearin' some kind of cloak. He said the guy stumbled through his back porch light and he saw the symbol. Like a crescent moon with crossed spears. Krantz said he pulled out his shotgun and threatened to shoot the guy, but he hardly responded. Didn't even look over, just kept walkin'. Krantz was so floored he never fired off a shot. Tell me that doesn't sound like some punk-ass kid in a gang, or high on something."

Jude took a deep breath. "Yea, it sounds like a gang," she said, knowing that it was not the kind of gang that Willie was familiar with. The symbol stirred Jude's memory. It sounded familiar and Jude was certain she'd seen it before. That night with Mr. McCormick in the cemetery. When she found his vacant grave, she noticed the symbol, but didn't recognize it as anything important. It was late, and she was ready to go home. Now she was kicking herself for not being more suspicious.

"The girls were from the same neighborhood. They lived on the same street," said Willie, pulling

Jude back into the bar room. "And they disappeared on different days. Whoever it is wasn't afraid to hang around. Which means he was stashing the first little girl somewhere."

"Samantha disappeared from a neighborhood park," added Jude.

"Yeah, which means the kidnapper was casing the place. He probably knew she'd be going there, and figured it would be easier to swipe her."

"So, you think that the two little girls were chosen for a reason. It wasn't arbitrary?"

Willie shook his head and finished his beer with a few hard guzzles. "I'm saying it's awful coincidental that both little girls were four years old and new to town."

Jude had been lifting her glass to take a sip, but stopped halfway. "They were new to town?"

Hank nodded. "Yeah, both only been here for a few months."

"I suppose the kidnapper followed them from wherever they were from,"said Willie.

"My cousin Donnie passed back in the spring," said Eddie. "Left the house to his son Tim. Tim moved his wife and daughter, Lacey into the house maybe six weeks ago. Tim can't stop talking about how he wishes he'd never moved here."

Jude's heart began to race. "I have to go, it was

nice talking to you guys." She slapped five dollars on the counter and ran out the door.

CHAPTER 10

When the headlights fell onto the front of the old farmhouse, Jude was relieved to find that all seemed at peace. She unlocked the door and went immediately upstairs, where Ezra was sitting at her desk on the computer, the door open and looking into Jude's room. A sliver of light fell over Shiloh, who slept soundly in her bed.

"Oh, you're back," said Ezra, looking up from her screen.

"Yeah," answered Jude. "How did it go?"

Ezra smiled. "Just fine. Shiloh did wake up once, but I told her that you would be home sooner if she went back to sleep."

Jude laughed. "And it worked?"

"No," replied Ezra. "Three picture books, two songs and about twenty minutes of back tickling worked. So, how about you? Did you find anything?"

Jude leaned in the doorframe, arms crossed over her chest. "I found out that Samantha and Lacey were new to town. Which makes me even more convinced that whoever took them was looking for Shiloh. But I also got this tip about a symbol. Some guys were saying that they saw it on the jacket of what he called a gangster."

"Did he say what it looked like?"

"A crescent moon and crossed spears. And I think I know where we might be able to find it. Come with me to the cemetery tomorrow?"

Ezra looked curious, but agreed. "Where'd you get all this information?"

"Henley's bar in town."

Ezra gave a deep nod. "That explains why you smell like liquor."

"Just reliving my youth," Jude said dramatically as she walked out of the bedroom. "Goodnight."

Jude checked all the locks in the house and then made her way back upstairs to go to sleep. The night was quiet and cool, and she wanted to open the window. She worried, though, that leaving it open may invite unwanted guests. The whole house had been sanctified and blessed by the Synedrion's ancient rituals and traditions. Amulets hung from ceiling hooks and crosses above doorways. But she didn't believe it was possible to be too cautious. Instead she closed the curtains, tucked Shiloh tighter under the covers and slipped into bed. But it was not a restful sleep. She tossed and turned as images of the little girls ran through her head. How had she been so stupid to ignore that symbol etched into the vampires tombstone? Why had she not considered that they were working for someone?

All night, flashes of nightmares kept her just on the edge of sleep. In them, she would be calling out to the girls in the dark, chasing them through a thick forest, crawling through a dark tunnel. The tunnel floor was hot. It was difficult to breathe. She could see an orange glow that she knew she had to reach, but just before she did, she was jostled awake, or worse, back at the beginning of the nightmare in the forest.

Jude began to fight the recurring pattern of the dream. Just as she was nearing the orange glow in the back of the tunnel, she would plant herself there, refusing to be sent back to the forest. To go back to square one. her conscious mind battling her unconscious mind, knowing that there was something behind that glow that would help her save Samantha and Lacey. It never fully worked, but each time, she managed to hold on a few seconds more before being sent back to the beginning of the loop. Finally, when she had made it back to the glow for the last time, she reached her hand into it. It felt like fire. She heard chanting. She could feel the dream begin to pull her back to that forest. She knew she couldn't fight her subconsciousness any longer. Just before she gave up, she saw it. Behind the flame. A giant, bull headed figure with horns and the body of a man. He sneered at her. Shot her an unsightly grin, and turned back to the fire. She was yanked from the tunnel, pulled through the forest, and shot up from her sleep, her two consciousnesses colliding together in the world of the waking.

When she opened her eyes it was morning. It was early, but the sun was up and Jude could hear birds singing outside. Shiloh had slept in her own bed through the night which was somewhat uncommon. Maybe that's why Jude didn't sleep as well. She got up and opened the window to sunshine and a comforting breeze. The air was clear over the mountains. The tall grass in the field behind her house was leaning against the wind, even yellower than usual in the early morning sun. The tree in the backyard, where Shiloh's tire swing hung, was still full with leaves but in full fall color, mostly orange and red, and starting to shrivel. On the far side of the house was a fence dividing their yard from the neighbors, whose house Jude could barely see. But behind the fence, the neighbors kept their cows, and Shiloh liked to go sit out there and talk to them. Of course, Shiloh wouldn't be going outside today. Not until the mystery of what was attacking little children in Acadia had been solved.

Jude walked downstairs and immediately turned on the news, hoping to find that no more children went missing in the night. Thankfully, she found that to be true. There were also no updates about the two that were already missing, just a short clip of Lacey's father asking for anyone with information to report to the Acadia police department.

Jude woke Shiloh and got her ready for school around seven thirty. Ezra rode along so that after they dropped her off they could go right to the cemetery. She waited in the car while Jude walked Shiloh inside, and on the way up the front steps, Shiloh paused suddenly and reached up to touch the cross fixed to the heavy wooden double doors of the building.

"See, mommy," she said quietly. "It's just like my necklace. Nothing can hurt me here."

Jude looked down at Shiloh, stricken with concern. "Shiloh," Jude knelt down beside her and put her hands on her shoulders. "Who would want to hurt you?"

Shiloh shrugged. "I don't know. Monsters and stuff." She paused and shuffled her feet. "You know about the monsters, don't you?"

Jude shook her head no. "What monsters, baby? Where did you see them?"

"They are in my dreams," Shiloh replied calmly. "But I know they're real."

Jude pulled Shiloh in. Nightmares apparently ran in the family. "Where else have you seen the monsters? Have you seen them outside of your dreams?"

Shiloh pressed her face into Jude's neck. Jude pulled her away by the shoulders to look into her eyes. "Shiloh, where have you seen the monsters?"

"Well, I saw someone. Last night." Shiloh stared hard at the sidewalk under her feet.

Kneeling on the church steps with hurried parents and their children all around, Jude scanned the horizon, looking for she knew not what. Maybe monsters. Maybe a sign. Maybe peace from the heavens. She got nothing. "Where last night?" she asked, forcing eye contact with her daughter.

Shiloh hesitated. "Outside. Before bed."

Jude's heart skipped. "Shiloh, you have to tell me about these things," she lectured. She knew she sounded more harsh than intended. "What did it look like?"

"A man," Shiloh said. "His clothes were black. He had messy hair. I couldn't see his face. He was taller than you."

"What did he do?"

Shiloh picked at her shirt. "Well, nothing," she said with a faint shrug of her shoulders. "He just stands there watching the house. Then he goes away."

"You've seen him before?" Jude felt a cold sweat running down her spine, and her face flushed with rage and panic.

"Sometimes," Shiloh answered.

Jude asked where she'd seen him standing.

"Around those big trees way out in the front yard," she answered, and Jude knew that she meant the stand of three oaks that were about fifty yards from the front of the house.

"Shiloh," Jude said sternly. "Are you sure you saw a man? You're not telling stories?"

Shiloh met Jude with her big blue eyes. "No, mommy," she insisted in her girlish voice. "I'm not telling stories. I saw the man."

Jude bowed her head and slid her hands down Shiloh's little arms to grab her hands. "I'm so sorry," she whispered, apologizing for more than Shiloh could possibly understand. "I will never let anything hurt you."

Shiloh smiled, totally unconcerned. "I know, mommy," she said sweetly. "In my dreams, you fight the monsters and they go away. And there are angels around me, so I'm not scared."

"Angels?" Jude asked. Shiloh had never been to church. Gideon attended and sometimes Jude would go, but Shiloh was much too young to remember. Maybe she heard about them in school.

"Yeah, angels," Shiloh smiled. Her blue eyes widened and her fawn-colored hair wisped in the wind. She put both hands on the straps of her pink Lisa Frank backpack and looked carefully at Jude. "They're big and have wings, and they glow, even when the sun is away. And they watch over me. You have them too."

"How do you know about these angels?"

Shiloh laughed. "I can see them, silly." She

reached out and wrapped her fingers around Jude's hand then began gently tugging her into the school. For a moment, Jude considered scooping her up, carrying her to the car and going home where she could watch Shiloh like a hawk all day. But she had monsters to find and destroy if she really wanted to keep Shiloh safe. Jude ran her hand over the heavy cross, just as Shiloh had done, and after a moment of pause, she exhaled deeply, and pulled the door open.

Jude took her daughter to her classroom and kissed her on the top of her head. "You tell those angels to keep you extra safe today, okay?"

Shiloh nodded then ran off to play. Jude lingered in the doorway for a moment until the teacher began attendance. Then she made her way back to the car where Ezra was waiting.

"My child says she can see angels," said Jude, exasperated as she climbed in the Jeep and buckled her seatbelt.

"Maybe she can," answered Ezra. "She is the chosen one, you know. Hand picked and designed by God and all. I wouldn't be surprised if she can see angels."

Jude shook her head in bewilderment, started the car and drove toward the cemetery. Her mind was all over the place; nightmares, visions, missing girls, strange symbols, and now, a stalker in her own yard. She probably would have been exhausted if she'd had a moment to think about it. One second, though, of surrender to the overwhelming flood rising within her spirit, and she feared she would never recover. She told Ezra about the stalker, and drove to the cemetery.

"The headstone was right over here," said Jude, leading Ezra through a maze of graves. Though she was a frequent visitor after dark, she hadn't actually been to the cemetery in the day. She decided she liked it better at night, when it was creepy and obscured. In the light of day, there was nothing paranormal about it. It was raw, shiney and exposed; an unpleasant reminder of human mortality.

Ezra seemed unphased. She walked smoothly with her hands in the pockets of her long brown coat, occasionally commenting on headstones. "Wow, this one is over a hundred years old," or "this whole family died in the same year." Then she would calculate ages and predict cause of death based on the age and historical period. Smallpox. Tuberculosis. Dysentery. War.

"Here it is," said Jude, her feet landing on spongy ground in front of Paul McCormick's grave. She knelt down, her knees sinking slightly into the cold, damp ground beneath them. She brushed away the loose dirt that had collected near the bottom of the headstone, and found the symbol. It looked like it had been scratched into the polished marble with a rock or a crude knife. Willie had described it well enough in the bar. It was a crescent moon, standing upright. From tip to tip was a long line, like a spear, and crossing that line was another shorter line. Ezra took a picture on her phone and sketched it down in the notebook she had brought along, and the two went home.

Jude stopped halfway up the driveway. With her fists balled tightly, she marched to the stand of trees where Shiloh said she saw the man. Ezra followed closely behind as Jude inspected the ground for any evidence. The tall grass had clearly been trampled and compressed under someone's foot, confirming that Shiloh was in fact not telling stories. Someone had been there. Before turning back to the Jeep, Jude looked up and toward the house where it sat a short distance away at the top of a small hill. She stood among the trees where someone inside would be unable to see her, and verified what she already knew and feared.

"Someone standing here can see right into my bedroom," she said as Ezra stood behind her and looked in the same direction.

"We'll find them," Ezra promised.

Once inside, Ezra pulled out her notebook and examined her sketch of the symbol. "So, how do we know that this has anything to do with the disappearance of the girls?"

"We don't," said Jude. "But we're sure hoping it does because that symbol means something and it's all we have."

Ezra nodded. "It looks old. The shapes are really basic, there's no real detail. Makes for quick and easy carving."

Jude sat down on the couch and pulled out her laptop. "I wonder if we will find anything on here," she said, as the screen lit up.

Ezra sat down beside her. "You can find anything on the internet."

The two spent an hour searching everything from academic papers to obscure blog pages, when finally something turned up. On a web page all about ancient symbology of the occult, they found their symbol. It was in a long list of other unnerving symbols, and the text next to it said only, "The Blood Ritual Symbol. Represents human sacrifice."

"Nothing about it's origins or who uses it today," said Jude, while Ezra looked closely at the picture on her phone and the picture on the screen. It was surely the same image.

"This looks like some kids blog. Who knows if any of this is even real?" asked Jude.

"Well, the symbols match," said Ezra.

"We're going to need more info."

Ezra pulled out her cell phone and began dialing a number. "I think I know someone who may be able to help," she said as she pressed send. "He's an old friend of mine, and he studies symbology. I don't know why it didn't occur to me sooner."

Jude leaned in close to listen when the person on the other end of the line picked up.

"Hey, Nigel, this is Ezra LeRoux from Lafayette."

Jude heard the man laugh and say hello.

"I'm doing well, how are you?" asked Ezra. there was a pause while he spoke. "That's great. Well, listen I'm actually calling for your help. I have this symbol I'm trying to figure out. I need information about it." There was another pause. Ezra described the symbol to him and nodded along while he spoke. "Well, do you know of anyone who uses it today? Groups or cults or anything like that?...Uh-huh.... Wow, okay." Her face became grave. "Well, it's just for a project I'm doing." She shifted nervously. "Yea, I'll be careful. I promise."

She hung up the phone.

"So?" asked Jude. "Any luck?"

"Yeah," said Ezra. "He said it's a blood ritual symbol. He said he wasn't sure of any groups that use it present day, but was used in Satanic circles to represent this one particular demon."

"Satanic?" Jude repeated. "Great. What demon?"

"His name is Molech," Ezra said quietly. "Apparently he was worshiped by Phoenicians and Canaanites. He's referenced in the Bible. He's some ancient Ammonite god."

"Well, let's learn a little more about this guy," said Jude, returning to the laptop.

"Wait," said Ezra. "He's a demon. I really don't think we should be typing his name into the computer."

Jude looked at Ezra puzzled.

"It's just that I don't want to accidentally invite this thing into the house."

"And demons hang out on the internet?" asked Jude.

Ezra shrugged nervously.

Jude looked back at the computer then back at Ezra. "Well, you're the expert. I do have some books we could try."

Ezra practically jumped off the couch. "Great!" she said. "Let's try the books first."

When Jude moved in, Gideon had taken her into the attic and shown her the books he'd put there.

Jude had not visited it since. But this was no ordinary attic. In Jude's bedroom, they walked over to the closet and stepped inside. It was dark, and there were clothes hanging in their path, but behind the clothes, Jude found the pull chain, and a light came on illuminating a wooden staircase.

"Wow," said Ezra quietly. "This house is awesome."

"Yeah, apparently whoever lived here stashed runaway slaves up in the attic on the Underground Railroad."

The unused plywood stairs creaked under their feet and dust clouded at their ankles with each step, but at the top, they found themselves standing in a long room, the roof pitched on both sides creating a triangular-shaped space. There was a round table in the center, and a red rug underneath it. All around were bookshelves, not entirely full, but with plenty of space waiting to be filled. One shelf, though, was filled with books. Ones with heavy, dusty and faded spines, bound in leather and burlap. Ezra walked near the bookshelf and brushed her hand over a round crystal hanging near it. The crystal swayed and moved the light that pierced through a boarded up octagonal window on the far side of the room.

"Oh, yea, Gideon loves his rocks," said Jude.

"It's not just a rock," said Ezra. "It's a gemstone. Tiger Iron. It's for protection from evil. Sometimes they're used in Rosaries." She looked around at the room and the crystals and gems hanging from the ceiling in every corner. "And over there is Agate and Ruby. Those protect children and families."

Jude nodded. "Someday this will be Shiloh's room. Right now, though, I think she's safest sleeping with me."

"You're probably right." Ezra scanned the bookshelf, brushing dust off the bindings, and pulled one out. The other books caved in in its absence, as books often do. "What about this one," she said. "It's called *Gods of the Ancient World*."

"It's huge," said Jude. "I hope there's an index."

They went to the table, and began poring through books. Ezra read through *Gods of the Ancient World*, and Jude flipped through another one that she had found: *Demonologists Compendium*. Of course, there was no index.

After about ten minutes of looking, Ezra landed on a page and pushed the book over to Jude. There he was: Molech.

She read the passage aloud. "Molech was worshiped in the region of Ammon, introduced therein around 7th Century BC. Known as Kronos in regions of North Africa. Molech was worshiped by many people across the middle east and into Africa and Levant, going by a different name in each, but known as Molech to the Phoenicians, Philistines and Arameans.

The first Biblical reference to Molech is in Leviticus where the Israelites were forbidden to make sacrifices to him. The nature of the sacrifice was as follows: an altar would be constructed to look like a man with a bull's head, and inside the statue was built an oven, where a fire would burn. On the arms of the statue, children were placed-" a knot caught in her throat. "Children were placed," she repeated. "And lifted into the fire in the pit of the altar's belly."

She quickly slammed the book shut and closed her eyes, but found no relief from the warm sour feeling rising in her stomach because with her eyes closed, she saw images of dark tunnels and raging flames. She saw the head of the bull and remembered. He was from the dream she had had the night before, but seeing him in print, she realized she'd actually been having the dream for some time. Maybe weeks. Trying to get to the bull-headed man. Fighting the heat that licked her skin. Being pulled back through the tunnel and dropped into the field, only to be forgotten by morning.

"This is our guy," she said definitively. She glanced down in disgust at the book before abruptly getting up from the chair and heading downstairs.

Ezra grabbed the book and hurried down after her. "Jude," she said, moving through the house. "Jude, are you okay?"

She found her in the kitchen pulling her shoes on.

"Hey where are you going?"

"It's almost time for me to go get Shiloh."

Jude looked pale and distraught.

Ezra put a hand on her back. "What are you not saying?"

Jude stood up from tying her shoes and leaned back on the counter. "I've seen that Molech guy in my sleep," she admitted, as if confessing to a crime. "I've been tired and feeling a little dazed and I should've known something was up. I've not been remembering my dreams, but I knew I was having them. Seeing his face, it made me remember. I've dreamed about him several times. If I was more attentive, I could have done something about this sooner."

Ezra shook her head. "No, there's nothing you could've done. And we still don't know that this Molech has anything to do with the missing kids."

"I am sure, Ezra. I saw him. I saw the fire. He requires child sacrifice. His symbol showed up in a little cemetery in a tiny, obscure town, then kids started vanishing. There are no coincidences." She was angry. Angry with herself, angry with whatever summoned this demon to town, angry with evil in all of its disguises, tricks and triggers.

Ezra exhaled and rubbed her hand over her forehead. "Alright, well, what is the next step?"

"Stay here," said Jude. "I'm going to go get

Shiloh from school. When I get back, we will make a plan. We need a location."

"Alright," said Ezra. "Well, be careful. I'll see what else I can find."

Jude walked out of the house and started the Jeep as her heart sank lower and lower into her stomach. She knew that it may be too late to save Lacy and Samantha, and couldn't shake the feeling that it was her own fault.

By the time she'd driven to St. Mary's, Jude had calmed down a little. She would get Shiloh home, and immediately go to work on a plan. There was no time to waste. She was beat, but she would have to fight it. They had to come up with a location. In her dream she'd seen a field, but in Acadia, Virginia, there were fields everywhere. She would need more than that.

Jude went into the preschool and picked up Shiloh, who was carrying a small painted pumpkin. "Look, mommy!" she squealed, running to the door of the preschool and jumping into Jude's arms. "Look, I made this for the porch!"

"I love it," Jude answered with a big smile, pushing all of her fears out of Shiloh's view. She carried Shiloh out of the school and strapped her into the car. Shiloh talked a mile a minute about her day and the books she had read and the things she had learned. She was excited for the upcoming Halloween party her teacher had mentioned, and already knew that she wanted to make jack-o-lantern cupcakes for her class.

"We're going trick-or-treating to every classroom," she said eagerly, playing with the plastic toy dragon that she'd left in her car-seat. Jude listened and chimed in when appropriate, happy to listen to Shiloh laugh and chatter behind her. Her voice was enough to offer Jude some peace.

When she was done with her story, Shiloh asked to listen to music. Jude turned on the radio and immediately tuned it out, flooded with thoughts of Molech. After a few minutes of obsession, she glanced in the rear view mirror and saw Shiloh swaying in her car-seat to the music. It was an old Billy Joel song, and by the second chorus, Shiloh had caught on to a few of the words and was mumbling along. When she was with Shiloh, it was harder for Jude to remain pensive and focused and angry. She had an uncanny way of melting all those unpleasant things away.

By the time they turned onto Peaks Street, it seemed as though maybe the entire world wasn't spiraling out of control. Maybe Jude could just enjoy a pleasant car ride with her little girl, singing along with the radio as fresh autumn air poured through the windows. For a fleeting moment, the threat of danger escaped Jude's mind and she breathed easy. In an instant, all of it was shattered.

Jude never saw it coming. She was half way through the second chorus when all of a sudden the

Jeep lurched to the side, out of control. Jude gripped the steering wheel but there was nothing she could do. She felt the impact, like charging into a wall, then everything went dark.

CHAPTER 11

Her vision was blurry. Her ears boomed and buzzed with the sensation of sitting too close to a speaker at a rock concert. She felt like she'd been hit by a bus.

Jude lay there, her breath somewhat labored. She heard people talking around her in soothing voices, but they didn't seem necessarily to be speaking to her. Somewhere close by, a siren or a horn was ringing, but nothing was coming in clear. There was a light above her that was far too bright, forcing her eyes shut just before the blurriness subsided. She shut them and sank into the pillow that was under her head. Why was there a pillow under her head? She was laying on something hard. Her mind was wandering, but she felt as if she was reaching through darkness, trying desperately to reconnect it with the real world.

"Ma'am," said the voice of what Jude determined to be a young boy. "Ma'am, my name is Jason. You're going to be okay. Do you remember what happened?"

Her head throbbed. She lifted her arm to rub her forehead, and felt something warm and wet. On the back of her hand, where she had touched her eyebrow, was a smear of fresh blood.

"What happened-" Jude echoed, still trying to orient herself. She felt nauseous, and an acidic vapor rose up from the back of her throat.

"Ma'am, you were in a car accident," said Jason.

A woman's voice asked, "Can you tell me your name?"

"What, no, I-" Jude spoke, but pain at the back of her neck forced her to stop. The fluorescent lights above her flickered and she could feel the buzz of an engine around her.

Her eyes opened slowly and she forced them to focus. A tall, teenage boy with pock-marked pink skin and red hair, presumably Jason, was standing beside her in an orange jacket. He had a clipboard in his hand. The woman, who was plump, with cold hands, was strapping a blood pressure cuff onto her upper arm. More came into focus. She was in the back of an ambulance. She looked around in a daze and saw that the large back door of the ambulance was still open and on the other side, she saw her Jeep, now facing the wrong way in the wrong lane, with a large dent in the driver side.

Finally, rapidly, it all came rushing back to her like cold water, arousing her from her dazed state.

"Where's Shiloh?" She spoke frantically. She

scanned the tiny space around her. Shiloh was not there. "Is there another ambulance? Where is she? I want to be with her."

The female medic placed her hands on Jude's shoulders to keep her still. "Please stay calm," she said. "You are in very good hands."

"No, where is my daughter?" Jude demanded, sitting up against the woman's pressure.

"I'm sorry, ma'am," said the boy nervously. "There was no one else in the car with you. You were in an accident, and you hit your head. Just lay back down and-"

Jude ripped the blood pressure cuff off of her arm and stood to her feet. The first few steps were a little wobbly. She felt sea sick. Her stomach rolled and her head spun, and as her focus came in and out, she lost her balance and crashed into the medical cart, sending metal implements flying and clattering around.

"Ma'am, please lay back down!" Jason urged.

The woman took a step toward her and pleaded with her to cooperate. "Are you sure there was another person in the car?" she asked.

Jude stabilized herself, refusing to sit back down on the gurney. "Yes," she answered. "My daughter. She's four. You don't know where she is?"

The medics looked at one another, confused.

Unwilling to wait, Jude pushed past them and jumped from the ambulance. Her feet landed on the pavement and jolted the pain in her head. The medics yelled after her but it didn't register.

Outside, the sun was bright and the wind was cold, and the Jeep was behind flashing blue lights, which Jude knew would be a problem, but she ran toward it, frantically calling Shiloh's name.

She threw open the back door and found Shiloh's booster seat empty. She was nowhere to be seen. Jude slammed the door shut and felt her breath catching in her lungs. She was falling quickly into an all-absorbing panic. She felt her fingers go numb, and the sensation ran up her arms and down her spine, leaving a frigid chill in its wake. She had to focus.

She leaned back on the Jeep to catch her breath, trying to slow the spinning as everything around her seemed to shift and run, like a still-wet watercolor. Without thinking she slammed her fist into the metal sidewalls and noticed something. In the back seat where Shiloh had been sitting was a small gold chain. She opened the door and held the fragile thing between her fingers. It was cool against her hand. Shiloh's cross dangled between the web of her fingers, and Jude felt her eyes well up with tears. She refused to break down. She slammed the door shut and leaned back against it, pulling herself together, repeating over and over: *focus. Notice. What do you see?* There were scraps of black paint on the Army

Green of the door where the car had been hit. She closed her eyes and thought hard. The vehicle that ran into her was large. It must have been black. Then it hit her. The vehicle that had been spotted casing Lacey McKinney's neighborhood the day she disappeared was a black Ford Explorer. And with that, Jude knew exactly where Shiloh was. And worse, who she was with.

Two officers in brown uniforms approached her, and she felt cornered. They stood in front of her, asking her questions, but she was in another place and nothing they said made it past her vacant face. Instead, their words bounced off her skin. She wasn't registering anything on the outside, all-consumed by the visceral, gut-wrenching weight in her stomach, the pulse and rush of her blood pumping hot, the unrelenting swirl of her mind as her entire being became saturated by fear, dread, and inescapable reality: Shiloh was gone.

The cops ushered her back to the ambulance, and she went willingly, knowing that she couldn't get past them, but that the medics were easy targets. She sat back down on the gurney and the medics wanted to strap her down, but she promised she would cooperate. They reluctantly agreed to let her remain free, and the cops walked back to the vehicle. Once they were completely out of sight, Jude took her opportunity. When the larger woman turned to set up a saline drip, she grabbed the boy by the back of the neck, shoved him into the woman, and dove from the ambulance.

Jude stumbled into the street and sprinted in the opposite direction of her Jeep, past traffic cones and police cruisers and tried to disguise herself in the confusion. She was not sure where she was going, but she knew she had to run.

So she ran, repeating to herself that the pain was an issue of mind over matter, until she came to the woods that lined the street. She knew the woods were several acres wide, and that she could hide out there and call Ezra. Leaning against a tree, her chest pounded and tightened and she gasped for air. Finally, unable to fight the acidic gurgling in her stomach, her body heaved and she dug her nails into the rough bark and threw up on the base of the tree. Sick heat rose up from her chest, coupled with cold chills down her spine and she could feel herself go clammy and pale. Determined to utilize every available second, she spat several times on the ground, wiped her mouth on her sleeve, and patted the pockets of her jeans for her cell phone, but found nothing. The gravity of the situation settled around her as she realized that it must've fallen out in the crash, and that she would have to get a hold of Ezra some other way.

The J&J Market was only a few blocks away from the sight of the crash. If she could make it there, she could use their phone and call Ezra. Jude calculated her location and took off in the direction of the grocery store. A small creek trickled through the forest where she walked, just inside the treeline so that she could stay out of sight. She stopped at the creek to clean herself up. The water was frigid and sobering when she splashed it onto her face. It ran red when she washed off the cuts and gashes on her arms. She was losing a lot of blood. Her body was covered in minor cuts and gashes, but two seemed to be the most threatening: one large slit on her upper arm that looked to have been caused by shattered glass, and one gash above her left eye. But there was no time to stop and administer any kind of first aid beyond the splash of cold creek water.

She went as far as she could through the woods, but eventually she had to cross the street. Anyone could see her. She would horrify children walking, neighborhood busybodies would be concerned. Worse, the police could spot her and force her into custody for fleeing the scene. But there were no other options. She hoped she'd cleaned up enough to make it into the store and get to the phone without anyone making too big of a scene.

She stood on the sidewalk, barely outside of the trees, and was preparing to step into the street to cross when she heard the screeching of tires. She turned to look, but didn't recognize the blue pickup honking its horn and heading straight for her–not until she saw the driver stick his head out the window. She wasn't even surprised to find that it was none other than Christopher Alleghiri.

She was about to run for it. He was among the last people she wanted to see, but it was too late. He was calling her name and waving her down. He came in flying and practically jumped the truck onto the sidewalk.

"Get in," he called.

She hesitated. "What? No, I can't, I-"

"I know, hurry up and get in, I'll take you home!" he yelled again, this time frustrated. He checked his rearview mirror and looked back at her. "Just trust me!"

She instantly weighed her options. Christopher was here now. If he refused to take her home, she could knock him out, toss him in the bed and steal his truck. With no better choices available, she pulled her weak and wounded body up into the vehicle.

He tore off the sidewalk and turned the truck around, away from the hospital and toward her house. He looked over at her, then looked away.

"Are you okay?" he asked after a short pause. "You look really rough. You do need medical treatment."

She waved him off. "Christopher, what is going on?" she asked impatiently.

He gripped the steering wheel and took a breath. "I've been looking for you," he answered.

"Looking for me?" Jude asked, only half-interested in his explanation. The searing pain all over her body was more distracting.

"Yes," he answered. "I heard about the accident. Someone saw it happen and it's making its way through town."

"Great," answered Jude as she pressed her hand against the cut on her forehead. "What does that have to do with you?"

Christopher was clearly contemplating something. He looked distraught and conflicted, like he couldn't decide between the truth, or a slight variation therefrom, but Jude was out of time, and out of patience.

"Christopher," she said curtly. "Out with it. What the hell is up with you? You have something to say, so just say it."

"I've been watching you," he answered finally, and Jude was taken aback.

"Excuse me?"

"Since you got here." He spoke quickly now, and guilty, like it all had to come out at once. "Remember that dream I told you about?" he asked.

"Yes," Jude answered, suddenly very interested.

"Well, I didn't tell you the whole thing." He

kept his eyes mostly on the road and drove ten miles over the speed limit, but occasionally glanced at Jude in the hopes that he could gauge her reaction based on her expression. She was hard to read.

"Go on," she said.

"In the dream, I saw you."

"You saw me?" she repeated.

"Yes, I saw you. And Shiloh. I didn't know who you were of course, but I saw you, and I knew you would be here, in this town. That's why I came. To find you. When you finally moved in, I had to know you. So, I've been watching you."

She had no idea if she should feel creeped out, betrayed or appreciative. She looked at him behind the wheel, in his black slacks and suit coat, his hair standing up from sweat. His eyes were a little wild, a little relieved.

"Have you been stalking us from the trees in the front yard?" she asked.

He looked embarrassed. "Once or twice, yes," he said, and suddenly Jude felt a little better about Shiloh's mysterious monster.

"So then you know who I am?" she asked.

He shook his head rapidly. "No," he answered. "All I know is that you are the reason I am supposed to be here. I'm supposed to help you. Whatever you are."

"And that's the truth? The *whole* truth?" If she was feeling better, she would've given him good reason to make sure he was being completely honest; something like a knife at his throat. Instead, she sat relatively helpless in the passenger seat.

"I swear, Jude. I would've told you sooner, but I was hoping to learn something first. Figure out how I could factor in."

"And did you?"

He sighed. "No, I didn't. What are you, exactly?"

She rolled her eyes. "I'm a person, Christopher. What kind of question is that?"

He backtracked. "No, I mean-"

"We don't have the time now," she said, more urgently. "Shiloh is missing."

Jude let out a loud exhale and propped her head against the window, sinking for a second into grief, trying to steady herself and prepare for what was to come, what she knew was going to be the worst hours of her life to date. They were almost home. This was all too much to process and she would have to work it out later, but for right now, Christopher was in on the action and there was nothing she could do about it.

They pulled into the driveway and Jude had the door open before the truck came to a stop. She climbed out of it and sprinted for the house with Christopher trailing behind. She flew through the back screen door and into the kitchen.

"Ezra!" she screamed at the top of her cracking lungs. "Ezra, where are you?"

Ezra came bounding down the stairs and into the room at about the same time Christopher made it through the door.

Ezra gasped and took a step back before running to Jude and taking her by the arm. "Oh my God, Jude, what happened? You are bleeding everywhere. You need stitches."

"Car accident," answered Jude, exasperated and leaning against the table, gripping her midsection. "Shiloh is gone. I know it was that demon who kidnapped Lacey and Samantha. I need to know where to look for them. I have no idea. They're somewhere in a field. Maybe under a field. There's a lot of fire." She reached back into the memories of her dream. "The walls are made of stone. It was like a tunnel or something. Please hit the books." Jude noticed the metallic taste of blood at the back of her tongue. She felt swollen and disconnected from herself. The kitchen light was forcing her eyes shut and the pain in her head had only gotten worse.

"Did you hit your head?" Ezra asked, stepping closer to get a better look. "Jude, you probably have a concussion, you should really-"

"Books, Ezra. Please."

"I don't know if the books are going to help us find them if they're local," answered Ezra as she cracked open a bottle of water. "We don't have anything on local history or geography." She moved to the cabinet and got a bottle of ibuprofen. Jude swallowed four.

The water helped a little and she began to hyperventilate for a different reason. "Ezra, I don't know what condition she's in. I don't know if she was hurt in the accident, or if they're hurting her now, and I don't know what they want with her. We have to find her. If anything happens to her I'll-"

Ezra cut her off and put her hand on Jude's shoulder, stabilizing her unraveling friend. "Alright, I know," she said. "We won't let anything happen to her, I swear."

Christopher, who had been standing uncomfortably in the kitchen watching all of this unfold, finally spoke up. "You should find a local historian. Maybe at the library or museum. I'll bet they would know something. Or have access to old maps." Ezra looked at him, noticing his presence for the first time. "Who the hell are you?" she asked.

Christopher cleared his throat. "Christopher Alleghiri," he answered, nervously.

Ezra looked at Jude, who closed her eyes and shook her head. "I'll explain later," she said weakly. "We're going to need weapons."

"Weapons?" Christopher asked, as the three went down to the basement.

Ezra followed Jude and loaded weapons into a duffle bag as she was given them. "So tell me everything you remember about this place," she said, as metal clanked off the brick walls and went into the bag.

"It was hot. There was fire. It was underground, in some stone building. It was dark, I got the sense that the place was old. It was in a field or forest something. Not near other buildings. There was a tunnel in the building that I kept trying to get through but every time I tried the dream would pull me back."

Jude gathered up all the supplies she could come by. She had an assortment of knives, crossbows and holy water stashed away. When the bag was bulging and couldn't zipper shut, she decided that was enough and pulled one more thing off the wall; a long dagger with a sapphire handle. She strapped it to her leg and carried the bag up the stairs, calling Ezra behind her. Christopher followed, clueless and bewildered.

In the kitchen, Jude downed two glasses of water.

"You cannot go anywhere until you do something about those cuts," Ezra demanded. "If you pass out, you will never be able to help Shiloh."

Reluctantly, Jude knew that Ezra was right. She agreed to sit down at the table and let Ezra do some quick bandaging.

"Christopher," she began, while Ezra wrapped a gauze bandage tightly around her arm. "Can we borrow your truck?"

"Of course," he answered. "But I'm not sure you should be driving."

"Ezra can drive," Jude responded.

"It's a manual," he said, looking at Ezra for confirmation, but she didn't offer it.

"I can't drive a stick," said Ezra, and Jude groaned.

"Fine," she said. "Christopher, you drive. But you cannot deviate from the plan. I swear to God, I will rip your still-beating heart from your chest if you try anything."

He swallowed a hard lump in his throat. "Yes, of course, I want to help."

Ezra finished with her arm, then moved on to taping up Jude's forehead. She squirted some kind of disinfectant onto the cut which burned like hell, then pulled the sliced skin together with medical tape and covered it with more gauze. It wasn't the best, and there were plenty of other injuries that needed attention on Jude's body, but time was up. They all climbed into Christopher's truck and it slid out of the driveway like it was on ice.

CHAPTER 12

"Where are we going?" asked Ezra, as the truck shifted through gears.

"We're going to take us a hostage," said Jude.

"Who?"

"I don't know, the first slobbering creature of the night we see."

Ezra paused. "Creature of the night? Jude, it's day. We're not going to find anything."

"They don't cease to exist in the day, Ezra. They hide somewhere."

"I'm sorry, what hides somewhere?" Christopher asked.

Jude looked at him. "Demons," she stated.

Christopher exhaled and kept driving forward.

"There is a disproportionate number of vampires to dead people in this town. So I know they're hiding out someplace," she continued. "They're coming here from somewhere else and making plans. They're setting up shop in this town because we're here. We just have to find the shop."

"Be careful, we don't want to get pulled over," said Ezra, as she watched the speedometer reach 70. "It will only slow us down."

Jude hated the idea of obeying traffic laws while Shiloh was God knows where, but once again, Ezra was right. If they were pulled over and she was seen by the police, it was over. She was now guilty of fleeing the scene of an accident. She asked Christopher to slow down as they came into town. Jude scanned the streets for any sign of unusual activity, but she wasn't entirely sure what she was looking for. Old abandoned buildings and exposed sewer accesses were her first targets.

"I wish I knew this town better," Jude said under her breath.

"Where have most of your kills been?" asked Ezra.

She racked her brain. "Most of them have been around Baltimore Avenue," she said. "The park and the cemetery there."

"There's an old, rundown industrial park that way," said Chris. "A lot of it is abandoned. It would make for a pretty good hangout for anyone wanting to be invisible."

"Well then that's where we want to start," answered Jude.

It had been seven nights since Jude arrived at Gideons house, four nights since the baby was dropped off by the Synedrion, and three nights since Jude saw the baby's DNA sequence compared to her own; saw that it looked identical.

The baby had been sleeping in Gideon's room, in an old cradle that he had picked up at a Goodwill. The crib in the room Jude had been given, white and solid oak, with intricate lace bunting and yellow flowered bedclothes, remained empty. Gideon had tried to force Jude and the baby together, but Jude resisted. Even after the blood testing, the journals, the undeniable proof that they looked like almost the same person, Jude couldn't accept it.

It was the fourth night, and the baby had not stopped crying. All night, every night, she would wail at the top of her lungs until she couldn't produce any more tears, then she would suck in air in short, mournful bursts until she worked up the energy to cry again. Jude could hear Gideon pacing around the living room with her in his arms, trying to lull her to sleep, or just calm her down. It wasn't like Jude was trying to sleep or anything. She couldn't sleep anyway. But she felt bad for the baby. She was taken from her mother, far from home, scared and alone.

Finally, she'd had enough. Jude ripped the covers off of her body and stormed downstairs. She found Gideon on the couch, bags under his eyes, the baby in his arms with her fists flailing in the air.

"Give her to me," Jude demanded.

Gideon looked at her cross.

"Just give her to me." Jude took the baby from him and laid her over her shoulder. Her sagging diaper molded around the shape of Jude's boney arm, and she carried her upstairs. Gideon watched her go, and even smiled a little as Jude stomped back up to her room as if she'd just lost a battle.

The baby was tiny. Only days old. Her fists were tight and her eyes were blinking from tears. Jude sat down on the edge of the bed and held her to her chest, unsure of what to do. She had not grown up around kids, and had very little experience with infants.

She sat there, on the edge of the bed she'd been lying awake in for four nights, in the cooling autumn breeze coming in from the window, in darkness subdued by one small shaded lamp on the bedside table, with a mortified baby in her arms. But the strangest thing happened; as Jude sat there, whispering to the baby words that meant nothing, she began to quiet. Her sobs pulled back into catching breaths, and her heart slowed to a more comfortable rhythm. Her eyes, reddened from crying, widened and Jude noticed the cerulean depth of them, staring back at her. The baby was soft and warm. She felt good in Jude's arms.

Jude rolled over onto her back and laid the now hushed and complacent baby on her chest. She reached over and extinguished the lamp on the bedside table, and just kept talking. The more she talked, the calmer the baby became, as if the sound of her voice was all she'd wanted all along. Jude reached back to the poetry she'd memorized in childhood, when her mother would read Shel Silverstein before bed, and began to recite the simple rhymes she remembered until the two of them drifted off to sleep in the still darkness. From then on, something was different. Jude thought of nothing other than the baby, waking up several times a night to check on her, to listen to the rise and fall of tiny breathing, to feel the raw, organic comfort of tiny fingers wrapped around her own. There was absolutely no question, Jude was falling in love for the first time in her life.

There was a large barbed wire fence encircling the industrial park, and inside was old pavement and brick buildings. Some of them had large cement towers looming toward the sky, many had broken and shattered windows and graffiti painted on the walls. Only a few were still in operation.

They did a spin through the area and one building caught Jude's eye. It was a large brick factory of some kind, long vacant. It differed from the others in that the doors and windows were all boarded up.

"Doesn't look like any sunlight could sneak in there, huh?" asked Jude, looking through the dusty truck window at the building.

"I'd say probably not," answered Ezra. "So what's our plan?"

Jude jumped out of the truck and grabbed her bag of goodies. "We go in there, tear it up a little, grab one or two of 'em and have a chat."

"That's the plan? The whole plan?" asked Ezra nervously as they climbed out of the vehicle.

"We have the element of surprise, Ez," said Jude. "That's all the plan I had time to make." She looked at Christopher. "You wait here," she demanded. "We will be right back."

Christopher nodded. He looked pale and terrified, gripping the steering wheel for dear life.

Jude ran her hands over a door that had been bricked in. There were windows lining the building that had been covered with plywood and other scrap materials. Several "Keep Out" signs were taped to the door. In one swift motion, Jude kicked through the rough brickwork, sending shrapnel of brick and mortar crumbling to the ground.

"Morning, folks," she said, arms crossed in a rain of brick dust. Light rushed into the dark room and sent hellion creatures clambering for the shadows.

The things were disoriented, having likely

been asleep when Jude and Ezra busted in. Jude took a large axe out of her bag and swung it through the plywood shield of a window. It made a pleasant popping sound and splintered. More light poured in and Jude caught a better glimpse of what she was dealing with.

"Think we found our lair," said Ezra, lingering by the doorway. Her tone was unsure and unconfident. She had never killed anything before, and certainly never interrogated a monster. She was nervous about all of the unknown variables, the lack of control, but Jude seemed to thrive in the chaos.

There were six or seven vampire-looking beings pinned to the far wall where the light couldn't reach. They snarled and showed their teeth, desperate to get at Jude and Ezra, but they were safe. Protected by the light.

These were not sleepers, though, and their threat could not be taken lightly. These creatures were older, more sophisticated, with bellies full of blood and strong muscles, cunning and coordinated.

"Say fellas, I think you and I have some things to discuss," Jude said, oddly calmly.

The vampires clawed into the light, and the air smelled of dust, mold and burning flesh. Jude could feel her throat drying.

All of a sudden, two vampires braved the sunlight and charged, one at Jude, the other at Ezra. Jude grabbed her attacker and his skin began to smoulder and smoke. He was writhing in pain but was doing his best to put up a fight. Jude glanced at Ezra and saw that the monster had her by the neck.

Jude swung and punched it in the jaw. It lurched back, but sprang forward again. Ezra cried out for help. Jude grabbed the vampire and ran, shoving it into the sunlight, right out into the parking lot. It squirmed and fought and in a matter of seconds, let out an ear piercing scream and turned to dust. Jude stood there in the open light of day, the dust of a dead vampire on the ground at her feet and hoped no one was around to notice. Christopher, of course, had seen everything from the truck and sat open-mouthed and speechless. Jude heard Ezra's screams again and rushed back into the building.

With the dagger on her leg, Jude locked her hand over the back of another vampire's shirt and plunged the dagger through its heart. It wouldn't kill him, she knew, but it was enough for Ezra to have room to pull out her stake. Ezra fumbled with the wooden stake awkwardly in her hands, rushing to find the right position. Finally, once it was poised in her grip, Jude pointed to the knife wound and Ezra buried it right into the hole that Jude had made, and the creature burst into dust.

Ezra caught her breath and Jude gave her a quick pat on the back then turned to the rest of the creatures. "So," she began. "Which of you sick freaks leads the pack?"

None of them budged.

Jude stepped closer, dagger raised above her head. "I will kill every single one of you right here if you don't start talking!" she yelled. "Who is it?" She was frantic, her heart racing, adrenaline pumping through her body.

"Still no one wants to talk?" Her voice caught from the screaming. She reached into the shadows and grabbed the smallest, most innocent looking of the creatures. When she pulled it into the low light it began to smoulder, and the pain must have been intense because it did very little to fight back. He looked to have been young when he died, maybe eighteen.

None of the others reacted or tried to get him back. "Cowards!" she shouted. "You're all cowards" She tossed the vampire onto the ground and stomped on its chest, pinning it to the sunlit floor.

For a moment, Jude felt herself go light. She felt dizzy, and things around her started to blur. As she lapsed, the vampire tried to wriggle out from under her but Ezra stepped in and pinned it back to the floor, smoke rising slowly from its body.

"Jude, are you okay?" asked Ezra. "You need to sit down."

Jude fought it off. "Kill him," she said to Ezra without taking her eyes off of the others.

Ezra hesitated.

"Kill him!" Jude yelled.

Ezra knelt down next to the defenseless monster and focused on it's chest rather than it's eyes.

"It's not human, Ezra! It's evil! Now take it out!"

Ezra plunged the stake through its heart.

"Three to go," said Jude playfully. A few deep breaths and she was steadied again. "Ezra, do me a favor and get ready to take out another window on my go." She handed Ezra the axe and Ezra approached the window closest to the cowering vampires.

Jude was on fire. Her whole body felt electrified, and the pain she felt only fueled her rage. Her blood ran cold and her fingers itched with the urge to rip the limbs off of the writhing animals.

"Now, here's how this works," said Jude. "You tell me who gives the orders around here or I'll tell her to bust that window wide open, and when she does, your little patch of darkness is going to get an awful lot smaller."

Ezra raised the axe to take out the plywood. Just as she was about to swing, two of the vampires pointed to the one on the far right.

Jude smiled a twisted grin. "Perfect," she said. "Ez, take out the window."

Ezra smashed the window out and light filled the room.

"Liar!" screeched a vampire as it began to smoulder.

Jude shrugged. "I'm not going to lose any sleep over it." She threw the two vampires further into the light and they burst into dust after letting out the same blood curdling scream as the first.

Jude found herself standing before the only vampire left. It was shoved back into a corner, in a few inches of shade.

"I like these odds much better, don't you?" Jude said to Ezra, who responded with a pleasant nod. Jude looked back to the vampire and gave it the once over. "You creatures disgust me," she said confidently.

She had Ezra guard the monster while she pulled an old wooden chair out of a room across the hall. The vampire watched as she pulled a rope from her bag. Jude got close enough to smell the vampire's breath and looked him in the eye. "I'm going to tie you up, and beat the hell out of you until you tell me what I want. It's up to you how long this takes."

The vampire growled and spat in Jude's face.

Jude punched him in the jaw.

She pulled the chair close and grabbed the vampire by it's jacket. "Sit down," she demanded as she threw it into the seat. "Ezra, help me tie him up."

The two of them wrapped the ropes around its body until they were sure he couldn't get loose.

Jude left the hellion tied up in the chair and walked casually to her weapons bag. "So," she said as she rifled through it. "What's your name? I'm Jude. You've heard of me, no?" She spoke with almost child-like civility. Ezra worried she'd gone mad.

The vampire jerked in his chair. "They call me Rock," he said in a deep, rolling voice.

"Rock," Jude repeated, her back still to the vampire. "Why do they call you Rock?"

He laughed. "Because I'm hard to break."

Jude smiled. She had laid out before her on an old wooden table an assortment of tools and implements of pain. She had never tortured anyone before. Torture was not exactly part of her training. As a retired Marine, Gideon called it "intelligence gathering". At the time, Jude assumed she would never be capable of torture. Now, with her daughter missing, her entire world teetering on the edge of a cliff, and a sub-human beast tied to a chair in a warehouse, she felt as if she had snapped, and the idea did not bother her. In fact, the thrill of it all flowered in her stomach.

Finally, she turned back to the vampire, a bundle of weapons in her arms. "Well," she said, kneeling before him and meticulously lining up her weapons on the cold floor. "Consider me a chisel." She cracked her knuckles. “Ezra, would you please keep an eye on the door?”

Ezra nodded but couldn’t conceal a nervous flash in her eyes as she moved toward the door. Jude knew she was out of her element. Ezra was definitely the bookish type. Not inclined to violence in any way. Jude was always a fighter.

Jude knelt down, rested both hands on the vampires lap and locked eyes with him. “I’m going to ask you a few questions. It is very important that you answer them quickly and correctly because every time you don’t I'm going to make you very, very uncomfortable.” She shot him a charming, half-smile. “So, here we go.”

Jude picked up the dagger and ran the blade over her hand. “What do you know about a demon named Molech?”

The vampire laughed and shook his head. “I’m not telling you a thing, sweetheart,” he said coolly.

Jude took the dagger and jammed it into his thigh.

The vampire let out a loud wail and skidded the chair back a few inches into the sunlight. When his skin started to burn, he yelled some more.

“Oh, I’m sorry, did that hurt?” asked Jude. “Let me ask again. What do you know about Molech?”

The vampire's face hardened and he stared at

the wall behind her.

"You've got nothing to say?" Jude swiftly took the dagger and turned it in the wound. Dark blood oozed out slowly. "How does that feel?"

The vampire gritted his teeth. "It won't kill me," he said. His flesh still burned and the air smelled rancid.

Jude nodded and let go of the dagger, the red handle sticking out of the vampires leg. "I'm counting on it," she answered. "Maybe I should give you a little backstory. Molech and whoever is working under him have something of mine. Something very, *very* important to me. I want it back, and I'm going to get it. You're going to help me." Jude pushed the chair further into the sunlight and more smoke rose from the vampire's body.

He breathed deeply and sweat poured from his brow, but he was still laughing. "If you get anywhere near them, they'll kill you."

"You think so?" asked Jude. "How would you know? You're obviously not high on their list of importance. Or you wouldn't be tied up here in a chair in an old factory with my friend and I, would you?"

He shook his head to toss off her nagging. "You're spunky, I'll give you that. But it's not enough. They'll tear a little gal like you to shreds."

Jude picked up a small bottle of holy water.

"Well, I think that's for me to find out," she said, gingerly opening the cap.

"If you don't pull my chair back into the shade, the sunlight will kill me and you'll never get your answer," said the vampire between labored breaths.

Jude glanced at the pointed sunlight shining through the holes in the wall. "Yes, but right here, the light is not too bright so it will be a slow fade. Don't you worry about that." Jude stood up and calmly walked behind the vampire, who struggled to look back at her. She grabbed his head in her arm, pulling it back by his hair, and with the other arm, held the bottle of holy water over his face. "Where is he?" Jude demanded, her knuckles going white. She could feel hot rage rising into her chest, and her heart was racing, like something had flipped a switch and she was on. "Tell me where I can find them!"

The vampire said nothing. Jude poured a few drops of the holy water into his eyes.

He screamed as his eyes sizzled like steak on a frying pan. "Tell me!" Jude demanded. "Tell me right now!"

"Go to hell!" the vampire yelled.

Jude got right in his face, close enough that their noses were almost touching. She breathed slowly. "Tell me what I need to know."

He didn't respond. Jude pried his mouth open

and shoved the bottle inside. With the bottom of her palm, she smashed his jaw shut, and the glass shattered between his yellow teeth.

She held his mouth shut while his face turned red and he thrust violently in the chair. After counting to thirty, Jude released his jaw and he spat the glass out onto the floor in a bloody mess.

"There's more where that came from," said Jude.

He was obviously weakened. His head hung low and his eyes were closed, and his voice was hoarse and quiet. "If I tell you anything, you'll just kill me."

"You're already dead, jackass," Jude retorted. "But I can make it go faster. If you tell me."

He nodded, and let out a whimper. He lifted his head and spat glass in Jude's face. Full of fury, Jude reached down and grabbed a wooden stake. She plunged it into his chest, missing his heart by a matter of centimeters.

He screamed again, this time his head falling back toward the ceiling. Jude glanced at Ezra who watched in horror as the vampire dripped blood from his leg into a pool on the floor.

"How are we doing, Ezra?" Jude asked, referring to the door.

"No sign of anyone," answered Ezra, her voice shaking.

Jude refocused her attention on the vampire. "I can miss about a thousand more times, Rock." She twisted the stake in his chest.

"Okay, okay! Stop! I'll tell you!"

Jude sat back on her knees and folded her hands in her lap.

"God, you're a sick woman," said the vampire. He breathed heavily. "There's a group of vamps from someplace out west. Came through a few weeks back, following some head honcho. They wanted to raise up the big dead guy, your Molech. They're holed up somewhere in the mountains. In an old furnace or something. That's all I know."

Jude stood up and put her hands on her hips, stake in hand. "What do they need to raise him?" she asked, dreading the answer.

"I don't know," he said, looking at the ground.

Jude took the stake and buried it below his right collarbone. Blood spurted out like a fountain. "Blood!" he cried. "Blood of some little girl. That's really all I know, I swear!"

Jude looked at Ezra frantic. "Shiloh," she whispered. "We have to go now."

As Jude ran to the table and began zipping up her bag, Rock started to backpedal. "My guys aren't with them," he insisted. "We showed up after, heard there was some buzz in town. We just came for the low hanging fruit, I swear."

He was pleading for his life, but without bothering to respond, Jude glanced back and threw her dagger at his chest. It spun end over end a few times before planting in his heart. He turned to dust quickly and the dagger fell onto the seat of the chair. Jude grabbed it and her bag, and turned for the door. She was only somewhat surprised to find Christopher lingering in the doorway, his face swept with shock and fear. She shook her head, and hurried past him, grabbing him and dragging him by the arm.

Offering no explanation, Jude led the charge back to the truck and headed for the Acadia Museum, in the hopes that they would find someone who could tell them about the old furnace.

CHAPTER 13

Jude had woken up every morning for several weeks to the same sight. The baby on her bed next to her, eyes wide open, but silent and happy. She would be greeted with a big, toothless smile. Jude loved that smile. In fact, she couldn't help but smile back.

She had been watching the news. There were no stories of missing babies. She couldn't help but notice as well that there were no stories about missing NYU drop-outs. Gideon had shown her pictures of her relatives; of her grandmother, and her cousin Jacqueline, who was originally intended for the job, but was killed before she got the chance. He had been drawing connections, tracing lines back into Jude's family tree. He had been explaining things about her past that she had never been able to make sense of.

She was starting to feel more comfortable around him. He was funny, and well-mannered. Never agitated or impatient. He had a routine which he would not break. He loved to tell Jude stories about her ancestors. At first, she believed none of them, but they were sounding more and more truthful the longer she stayed with him. But a few weeks was not enough to erase a lifetime of history. Not enough to convince her of a huge destiny that seemed impossible.

On one particular, stormy day, thick, dark clouds hung low overhead and threw shadows all over the hills of Gideon's farm. The occasional rumble of thunder or flash of lightning kept Jude's attention focused on the sky. Gideon had tried to get her to come in for training, or history lessons, but she couldn't. There was some kind of static, an electricity that Jude felt in the air that day, and all she wanted to do was sit on the porch and wait. She felt different. She knew something was coming. Something was about to change.

She kept the baby close by in a little bouncy-seat on the porch. Jude sipped sweet-tea and watched the clouds move past. They were skating quickly through the sky, one replaced immediately by another. A light steady rain fell and made pinging sounds on the tin roof of the porch above her head. The rain washed out the image of the farm in front of her, making everything blurry and gray.

Suddenly, Jude heard the shrill, loud ringing of an alarm somewhere in the distance.

"Jude, come on inside," said Gideon. "That's the tornado siren. We need to get downstairs."

Jude stood up off her seat and moved to the edge of the porch. A sudden gust of wind ripped through her hair and pulled the strings of her hoodie back behind her. The sky had transformed into a deep green color. The color of a sunlit lake on an over-ripe summer day. Like the color she remembered from her childhood, leaning over an out-

board motor in a puffy lifejacket, her father holding onto her skinny arm, pointing to sunnies as they popped their lips out of the water. The alarm sounded again.

"Tornado warning, Jude, come inside," said Gideon, more forcefully. "Let's get to the basement."

Jude picked up the baby and the seat, and rushed into the house as hail shattered on the tin roof.

They were waiting in the basement with an old transistor radio, coming in on mostly static. There had been tornado warnings issued for half of Indiana, and Jude could feel the heat being sucked from the dank basement room. The baby was back in her seat, sitting quietly near the center.

Nothing preceded it. No burst of thunder, no popping or clattering, but all of a sudden, the lights went out. They had forgotten to bring a flashlight down into the basement and there was nothing around them but pure black darkness. Jude began to tremble. There were no storms like this in New York, and she was not used to this kind of waiting.

"Nothing to worry about," said Gideon, sensing her unease. "We're safe down here."

She sat on the cold cement floor and pulled her arms into her chest.

After a few minutes, the lights flickered back on. Jude exhaled and looked around the room. The next feeling that came over her was a different kind of terror. One unlike anything she'd ever felt. The baby's seat was empty. She was gone.

Suddenly, everything Gideon had said about the baby being special, about the forces of evil being after her, her life being in danger, it all became true in an instant. Jude's heart jumped out of her chest.

"Gideon, where's the baby?" She panicked, already standing and searching the basement. "Where is she?" she asked again, before he had time to respond. She could feel heat rising in her chest. She was terrified at the thought of the loss of that baby girl.

Something carnal rose up inside of her and she began moving boxes, looking behind things, hoping she just managed to roll out of sight. Out of nowhere she felt Gideon's hands grab her shoulders. "Jude, stop," he said loudly but with a certain sweetness. "She's fine, she's right over here."

Gideon pulled Jude to the opposite corner of the room where he had moved the baby while the lights were out. "I was worried she may get stepped on in the dark, so I picked her up and put her in the corner, that's all."

She was laying happily in her seat, examining a sock that she had pulled off, but that still held the shape of her tiny foot. Her blue eyes were as wide as always, unphased by the tension in the room. When she saw Jude, she smiled and reached both of her arms toward her.

Jude fell to her knees and scooped her up. She held her to her chest and felt their two hearts beating together.

She felt the babies warm, wet breath on her neck, and smelled the familiar smell of her hair and silky skin. Her heart melted and her anxiety vanished, replaced by relief from someplace new and unusual inside of her. That's when she knew for sure. There was no question, this was her child. And she would do anything for her.

Once in town, they pulled the truck into the parking lot of the history museum. It was a very small, old building and the door was heavy with chipping red paint. She pulled it open and the room smelled musty. It was quiet but voices could be heard from the back room.

"Is anyone here?!" Jude said shouted through a cracking voice.

Ezra put her hand gently on Jude's shoulder. "Let me handle this one," she said softly.

Someone poked their head through a doorway and smiled. "Oh, how wonderful," said a scrawny old man in a sweater vest. "It's been such a slow day. Please sign our registry." He pointed to a pedestal with a notebook on it. A pen dangled from a chain at its side. "All the exhibits are upstairs. We have-"

"Actually, we're just here for some information," Ezra interjected, gently.

The man put his hands in the pockets of his khaki pants. "Oh," he said, somewhat disappointed.

"What can I do for you then?"

As Ezra prepared to answer, a woman stepped out of the same back room. "Oh my goodness," said a bubbly, familiar voice. "It's Jude! It's so great to see you here!" said Mrs. Overstreet, moving quickly toward them. "And with Christopher, no less!" She gave Jude a not-so-subtle wink.

Jude rolled her eyes.

"How are you doing? Who's your friend?" Mrs. Overstreet injected herself into the meeting, nodding towards Ezra.

Jude ignored her and looked back at the man. "We're looking for some old furnace or something."

Ezra stepped forward slightly and spoke sweetly, masking the urgency. "Jude and I were looking to do some sightseeing this week, and we heard about an old furnace in the mountains. Can you tell us anything about that?"

The old man nodded. "Oh, yes," he said. "It was opened in about 1726 and closed around 1864. It was used to cast pig iron into-"

"How about a location?" said Jude anxiously.

Ezra looked at Jude patiently. "It's just that we are trying to get there before we lose the sunlight. Sorry," she said with a smile.

Jude stood behind her, hands against the podium bracing her overheated and exasperated body.

"Jude, honey, you don't look so good," said Mrs. Overstreet. "Do you want to sit down? Maybe have a drink of water?"

Jude shook her head. "No thanks," she said between breaths. "I'm just a little tired is all. So, where is this furnace?"

The old man scratched his head. It's off of Powell Gap Road on the Blue Ridge Parkway. It's a real windy dirt road, though. Be careful if you kids go down there. There's only one or two houses on the way. It's pretty desolate."

Ezra nodded. "Thanks, we will," she promised, and they hastily turned and went back to the truck, leaving Doris and the old man whispering behind them.

The drive felt like hours, though it was only about twenty minutes down the Parkway. Still, plenty of time for Jude to envision all the terrible things that could be happening to Shiloh. The road was built along narrow mountain ridges, offering breathtaking views of the surrounding mountain ranges, and valleys spotted with small communities. It drew thousands of tourists to the area every year, especially in the fall. It probably would've made a perfectly relaxing afternoon, maybe with a picnic, or short nature hike. But Jude hardly noticed the landscape; she was hardly aware of her surroundings at all. The only thing on her mind was Shiloh.

"What if they've got her trapped somewhere and she can't breathe?" said Jude through hands over her face. "What if it's dark and cold and she's alone? What am I saying? She's not alone, she's with indescribably horrible creatures who want her dead, she'd be better off alone."

"I know, Jude, but we're going to find her." Ezra answered, with an arm around Jude's shoulders as she sat squished in the middle seat.

"I have one job, Ezra. One damn job, to keep her safe. I failed. How could I have been so stupid? I should've kept her home from school. I should have locked her away until we found and destroyed the thing that took Samantha and Lacey. Why didn't I do those things? I knew as soon as the first girl went missing that this was about Shiloh, I just refused to believe it- damnit!" She punched the dashboard in front of her, which reminded her of all of the pain she was still in from the accident.

Ezra grabbed her fist and pulled it onto her own lap. "Jude, we are going to get Shiloh back, and we are going to stop whoever or whatever took her from ever hurting her, or another child, ever again."

"Ezra, what if it's too-"

"Jude, no," said Ezra fiercely. "Stop thinking like that. She is going to be okay, I just know it."

Jude nodded and took a deep breath. The seconds that passed felt like lifetimes."I know. I know she's okay. I would feel it if she wasn't. I would know. Right?"

"I think so."

Christopher sat quietly in the driver's seat, shifting gears, watching for road signs and generally staying out of it. Jude looked over at him and thought she'd take the opportunity to let him in on the dire circumstances.

"Shiloh," she said weakly. "She was kidnapped during the car accident. The... thing... that crashed into my Jeep was after her."

"Why?" Christopher asked innocently.

"She's special," Jude answered. "She can give them something they need."

"What's that?"

"Power." Jude ran a hand through her sweaty hair.

Christopher looked absolutely confused. "And that thing that you killed in the warehouse? W-what was that?"

Jude exhaled and Ezra leaned forward to answer him. "Your mom was wrong. Monsters are real. They're just not hiding under your bed."

"Vampires," Jude clarified.

Christopher took a slow, deep breath and

shook his head in shock. "And the vampires, for some reason, want Shiloh because she can make them powerful?"

Jude continued to look out the window with her head resting on the glass. "It's her blood," she said, matter-of-factly. "Shiloh isn't like other kids. I never gave birth to her. She was created by a group of religious people, using my DNA and other things."

"She's not yours?" he asked.

"She's mine," Jude answered confidently. "I'm her biological mother."

"So she's like a clone?"

"No, not exactly," Jude answered. "She isn't *me*. The other half of her DNA, the part that would normally be supplied by her father, is divine. A genetic code created centuries ago and protected by the most secluded, sacred arm of the Synedrion. They're practically divine themselves."

She spoke slowly, almost casually, like this wasn't all that unusual. If she'd had any energy at all, maybe she would have explained it with more color, more detail, but it was all she had in her to form coherent sentences. Ezra listened to the story too, even though she already understood, maybe more than Jude herself, how Shiloh had been created. Jude's tone was simultaneously endearing and angry, nostalgic and pained. Her heart had been pinned to her sleeve and she didn't have the strength to conceal it.

"Every few centuries, a child is called from my bloodline," Jude went on, as her breath fell foggy onto the window glass and quickly evaporated. "Always a girl, always created in secret, with ancient rituals and divine intervention. She's carried by a surrogate until birth, when she is delivered to the next Guardian in line, in this case, me. She comes to restore the balance of good and evil. She isn't a savior, that's apparently already been done. But she levels the scales when humanity starts to lean toward corruption and darkness." In her head, she heard Gideon's voice, when he used nearly the exact same words to explain it to her the day before she met Shiloh. "So if you weren't certain the world had gone to hell, Shiloh's very existence is proof-positive."

Christopher shifted in his seat. "I don't understand," he admitted, glancing at Jude, then focusing again on the road ahead. "How could she do that? Level the scales?"

Jude absently let out a cold, sharp laugh. "She dies. Isn't that how it always works?"

There was a heavy, breathless silence in the truck and Jude's damp eyes collided with Christopher's, then Ezra's.

Ezra slid her arm through the bend at Jude's elbow. When she did, she felt the quiver of Jude's muscles, the heat of her blood, and the trembling weakness overtaking her whole body. She squeezed tightly.

Jude cleared her throat and continued. "When she turns eighteen," she almost whispered. "That's when she'll fulfill the prophecy. Which is just a nice way of saying that's when she will sacrifice herself for the dumpster fire that is humanity. I'm just supposed to keep her alive 'til then." She used her free arm, the one that wasn't being held by Ezra, to quickly brush away an errant tear.

"The thing that took her," Ezra picked up, pulling Jude into her side. "It wants her blood to bring back some demon. Pretty much everything evil wants Shiloh dead."

"So she can't fulfill her destiny," said Christopher, reaching an understanding.

"Right," answered Ezra. "We're hoping to find Samantha and Lacey in the furnace, too."

"Well, we will," he said confidently. "We'll get all three of them back. We won't leave until we do."

Jude offered a faint, fake smile and then went back to looking out the window.

Christopher turned the truck down Powell Gap Road. *Desolate* was a fair word to describe it. There was no civilization save for a weathered ranger station and hiking trail signs. The road was darkened by shade from tall, ancient trees and it wound down a very steep slope, gravel spitting up and stinging the side of the truck with every turn. The tires slid slightly on the loose rocks. There were countless blind turns, and though the right side of the road was lined by the upslope of the mountain, the other side looked, guardrail free, over the edge, peppered with rocks and knotty tree roots holding fast to the plunging slope.

Jude decided then that if Shiloh was not okay, she would come back to this spot and simply shoot the truck off the side of the mountain, her inside of it, and there her troubles would end.

CHAPTER 14

At the bottom of the mountain, they drove over a bridgeless creek and found level ground. The road became less exciting, but more eerily empty as it came into a darker, thicker part of the forest. From a slightly elevated position, Jude looked down and could see what appeared to be a small stone pyramid with the point chopped off, leaving a flat top.

"I think that's our furnace," she said. "Stop the truck here."

Christopher pulled the truck off the road, gravel rolling under the rubber tires. "What's the plan?" he asked.

"They probably have some kind of guard. I don't want them to see us coming." Jude reached back and grabbed her weapons bag from the back seat. "I'm going to slip down the mountain and hopefully take out the guard before anyone notices me." She looked at Ezra, her blue eyes wide and alert. "If I'm not back here in three hours, go home and call Gideon."

Ezra laughed, then realized that Jude was serious. "Wait, no," she said resolutely. "I'm coming in there with you."

Jude shook her head. "It's too dangerous, I can't-"

Ezra grabbed a crossbow from the back seat. "It's not up for debate, Jude, this is the whole reason I'm here. Now we're wasting time."

"I want to go, too," Christopher retorted.

To this, Jude aggressively refused. "No way," she said. "Sorry, but not only am I not risking your life, I'm not going to have you slowing us down."

"I won't," he answered. "I could be useful."

"Can you even fight?" Jude asked.

"A little," he answered. "I can hold my own. Plus, I've studied demonology and exorcism. I could help protect you while you find Shiloh and the girls."

Jude exhaled slowly and closed her eyes. There was simply no time to argue. "Okay," she whispered. "Get out of the truck silently. Wait here for me, I'm going to walk down the ridge and see if I can spot anyone.

Ezra and Christopher waited from the safety of the truck as Jude moved silently down the road. The day was uncomfortably calm. It was a crisp October afternoon, and the sun was beaming through the orange leaves, leaving deceivingly beautiful pools of sky splashed on the path before her. Birds were singing, and the forest was deep and hardwood, full of tall, sturdy trees and blackberry vines. The air smelled loamy and damp, like forests often do, and Jude kept having strange flashes of the one summer she spent at

Camp Walden in upstate New York.

The camp was on Lake George, and Jude was sent there when she was about eleven. She spent half a summer there, in a cabin with four other girls her age. They went hiking and canoeing and swimming, did arts and crafts, built fires, and learned outdoor skills. Jude remembered it fondly, as being one of the few times in her life when she was truly at peace. The forest was still. The lake was like glass. Everything seemed to come together there so seamlessly and she felt that her life was a part of that. The open air, space to run, troubles arising and being so quickly dissolved by muddy lake water and the limitlessness of nature. In those weeks, she felt she understood life better than she had before. At the ripe old age of eleven, she understood that life was a wheel that kept on turning, ceaselessly engaged in moving forward, leaving the past behind. That wheel, she felt, could take her anywhere.

Someone took a long, fat stick and jammed the spokes. The wheel stopped turning. Without Shiloh, there was nowhere to go. Dead in her tracks stood the guard, like a sentinel, a long spear in its hand. Its back was to Jude, and it stood in a small clearing right before the entrance into the furnace. As it began to turn, Jude dashed behind a rock and watched its routine.

Its face was twisted into gnarls and lumps. It didn't see her, but she watched it closely. It paced ten or so steps toward her, scanning the area, then turned back around. It wasn't human. It wasn't a vampire. This was something else.

Quickly and quietly, Jude snuck back to the truck and whispered. "I saw it." She spoke rapidly, her breath rushing from her lungs. Its presence confirmed that they had found the location. Jude pulled Ezra and Christopher down to crouch below the truck bed. "I think there's only one. It's standing right out in the open."

Jude was practically hyperventilating. Urgency was rising inside of her and her mind was all over the place. Ezra watched her eyes shoot all around the truck, bouncing occasionally off of Ezra's and then back into the woods. "We have to move fast," she said, reaching for the crossbow on the ground.

Ezra grabbed her wrist. Unintentionally, she felt Jude's pulse beating under her skin. It felt like a tiny jackhammer pounding under her fingertips. "Let me do it," she said softly. "You need to catch your breath before we go in there or we will end up getting hurt."

"Ezra, no, if you miss-"

"I won't miss. But you might, you're shaking. If you rush into anything, or draw attention to us, we will go down. And think about what will happen to Shiloh."

Jude met Ezra's eyes. This girl was always surprising her. Her touch was soft but her bite was tough. Jude ducked her head down and rested it briefly in her hands. She took another deep breath and exhaled slowly, feeling a crushing sensation in her chest. Ezra was right. If Jude took the shot, she would miss and their cover would be blown. Ezra was a good shot. She performed superbly well in training.

"Alright," she said finally. "You can do it." Jude sucked down a few large gulps of water from a bottle and they made their way back to the rock where Jude had watched the guard move before.

Ezra gasped when she saw the face of the monster. "What is that thing?" she asked Jude, her voice lower than a whisper.

"I don't know," Jude shrugged. "It's out in the sunlight, so it's not a vampire. Could be some kind of demon. I'm no expert. But it's not human, and that's all we need to know. Shoot him down, Ezra."

Ezra placed the crossbow on the rock and steadied it. She let out a breath slowly and focused all of her intentions on the tip of the arrow and the heart of the creature at the bottom of the hill. Gingerly, with Jude white knuckling it behind her, she pulled the trigger.

The arrow shot cleanly through the woods and cracked into the chest of the guard. Ezra paused for a moment, satisfied with her hit, and looked back at Jude, who gave her an eager thumbs up. The guard fell to his knees and looked around the woods furiously. But his rage was short lived, and he fell on his back. He let out a shriek of pain and then fell silent, stilling after squirming on the ground.

Jude moved to stand up, but Ezra pulled her back. "Wait," she whispered. "Let's make sure there's no one else."

After a silent few minutes of crouching behind the rock, no one came to the fallen guard's aid. "I think we're good to go," said Ezra, releasing Jude's arm and standing to her feet herself.

As tactfully as possible, they scuttled down the side of the mountain, trying to be aware of their footing, while sliding on damp leaves and underbrush. Christopher kept up as well as he could and moved with all of his awkward, untrained and boyish limbs. They made it to the body of the guard, where Jude looked it over and decided that it was definitely dead.

They approached the entrance to the furnace. The building was much larger than it had looked from above. It was made from huge squared stones, some of which were missing or crumbled, leaving dark holes patching the structure. Vines, weeds and moss had grown up around the walls and forced their way into the cracks between stones, giving the entire archaic building the look of a lost temple or ruin of some long-gone native tribe.

The doorway was more like a triangular shard taken out of the side of the wall, tall and wide enough for people to walk through in pairs. The room that they stepped into was dark and empty. It was square, and slightly angled in, and the floor under them was made of dirty stone and coal dust. Jude felt her hand along the walls until she found a tunnel. She motioned for Ezra and Christopher to follow her, and they started down the pathway that seemed to lead under the mountain.

It was warm in the tunnel, much warmer than the chilling October air. The walls were warm to the touch. The tunnel took a slight turn to the left, and at the height of the turn, Jude could see a glow coming from the far end. She could hear the sounds of muffled voices, and what sounded like work of some kind being done. The clap of stones on stones and the clinking sound of metal echoed and reverberated through the tunnel.

Jude put her bag down. She opened it up, and loaded herself down with weapons: the dagger on her leg, two stakes in the inside pocket of her jacket, a crossbow slung across her back, a knife in hand.

"Take whatever you want," she said to her ragtag troop. "I don't know what we're going to find on the other side of that light."

Ezra dug through the bag and pulled out an arsenal for herself. Christopher pulled out a wooden cross, holy water, and a bowie knife. Silently, they advanced toward the light.

Nothing could have prepared Jude for what she would see inside.

The room was large and cavernous, and everything was glowing in a red, shifting light. They stood at the doorway unnoticed by the fifteen or so vampires who pushed wheelbarrows and swung hammers. They all seemed to be driven by something, working to finish a project. There was one being, dressed in a man's clothes, wearing a man's face, orchestrating over all the vampires, yelling at them, telling them what to do. He screamed orders at them, insisting they move faster. In the center of the room, a huge inferno rose almost to the ceiling. The vampires were working tirelessly, throwing fuel into the fire, their skin burned and raw.

They inched from the entryway to a more hidden area behind a wall, where they took in the scene. The thing directing the vampires moved over to a small table at the far side of the room, and on the table sat a thick, open book. He began to read something aloud but it was inaudible over the cacophony.

“I don’t see Shiloh, do you?” Jude asked nervously. She was taking in the number. The odds were not in her favor.

Ezra shook her head. “What are we going to do, Jude? We can’t just bust in there. We will be easy to spot."

Jude looked frantically around the room for a plan. There weren't a lot of great options. "Those look like vampires," she said. "I think I can grab one or two of them. If we dust them, we can steal their robes. Maybe we can disguise ourselves?"

"Our faces?" said Ezra doubtfully. "We don't look like vampires."

Jude crouched down and rubbed her hand against the ashy floor. It came back black and grimy. "They all look filthy," she said. "We will rub this on our faces. Keep the hood up. It's the best I can do, but I need to get in there to find Shiloh. We can't move from this spot dressed like this."

Ezra reluctantly agreed, and they waited for the opportunity to snag a vampire from the crowd. Finally, one walked closer, moving a wheelbarrow to collect from a large pile of coal. Discreetly, Jude reached her arm out of the darkness, pulled him in, and slapped her hand over his mouth. Before she staked him, she ripped his robe off, so it wouldn't get dusted with him. He was weak and hardly even fought back. With the robe in her hand, she staked him through the heart.

"One down," she whispered, handing the black robe to Ezra. Moments later, another being made the same attempt at getting coal and Jude gave him the same treatment. She tossed the robe to Christopher and they began covering their faces in the soot while she waited for one more vampire.

In a matter of seconds, a third vampire lurched over to the coal pile. Jude reached out to grab it, but she had gotten confident and relaxed her speed. The vampire reacted and dug it's dirty nails into her wrist. She squealed, then suppressed the pain as she thrust her arm away from the monster and brought it back up to collide with its chin. Before it had time to back up and go squeal to the others, she grabbed it by the neck while Ezra came up from behind and slipped the belt from her robe into its mouth. While she held it back, and Christopher watched in horror, Jude tore off the robe then sunk her stake into his heart.

She pulled the robe over her clothes and covered her face and hands with the silty black dirt, and pulled on the hood.

"One at a time," she whispered. "I'll go first. Count to thirty then follow me. Chris, you after Ezra."

They nodded and Jude slipped out of the corner and took up the wheelbarrow that the dusted vampire left behind. She smugly disappeared into the crowd of other black-robed vampires and began dumping loads of coal into the flames.

Right on time, Ezra came up behind her and dumped a load of coal into the fire. They made eye contact, before Jude turned to get another load. She passed Christopher on the way.

The fire was so hot that Jude could feel her skin blistering from ten feet away. Each dump of coal nearly suffocated her. She was so thirsty by the third load that she felt she may pass out. The vampires seemed unphased by it, either having skin thick enough to bare it, or having been doing it for so long they no longer felt the sting.

Just as Jude was wishing she'd come up with a better plan, the thing with the book raised his arms over his head. He yelled something and all of the vampires came to his attention.

"It is time, my brothers!" he yelled. "Your hard work is about to pay off. We are all about to be in the presence of true power!" His voice echoed above all the noise from the raging fire. "Bring in the child!"

Jude's eyes shot around the room to find another source of entrance and when she did, she found two vampires limping into the shifting light, out of a darkened corner of the room. They seemed to be dragging something behind them.

They were standing too close.

She couldn't see.

Jude moved to get a better view.

They were dragging a chain. She could hear it rattling on the floor.

Ezra shot a look at her, begging with her eyes for Jude to remain composed, but Jude didn't see it.

Her mind was more focused in that moment than it ever had been. Waiting for the vampires to separate. Waiting for the chain to reveal what was on the other end. Waiting for...

Two months had passed since Jude had been brought to Gideon's house. She was settling into the idea of motherhood and her destiny. It still took her by surprise all the time, and there were still plenty of moments when she felt like it was all insane. Like she was being played. Or like she was in the middle of a really long dream. But then something would always happen. The baby would cry and she would go running, that intense, ancient maternal instinct rising in her chest. The baby would smile and Jude would smile, unable to conceal it. The baby would make a new sound and Jude would be overjoyed; proud of her daughter's accomplishment.

So while the need to escape, to be returned to the "real world" was less and less consuming, a different problem continued to press at Jude's door. Gideon would bring it up from time to time. Not nagging, unhurried, but intent on reminding her that it must be done.

"What are you going to call her?" He would ask, peering over his glasses at the two of them, lost in each other's identical eyes.

Jude was always distraught by the thought of naming her.

A name is such a big deal. It's such a powerful

thing. The right name can get you through a lot. Jude knew that. She'd been given a good name. Really, it just meant that her dad was a Beatles fan. But for her, personally, it was a strong name. One given, historically, to boys. But she could handle it. It was a name she could hold on to. A name she didn't mind fighting for. She was complimented on it often. It was a good name, and it suited her well.

This baby needed a name much bigger than that. Her name had to have real power behind it. More than just a feeling. This baby deserved a name that would stand up to as many hard times as she would face, one that would tell people, before they even knew her, that she was important. She needed a name that would carry her. Give her strength when it was hard to muster. She needed a name that would remind her of who she was.

The pressure had mounted. Jude had a serious task ahead of her. It was not a decision she was prepared to take lightly. The baby was over two month old, and still called simply: the baby.

One morning in November, Jude was in the study with Gideon, pouring over old religious texts about theology and the history of Christianity. He said that it was God who called on Jude to protect his most prized creation. Jude hadn't been raised in a religious household. She had no faith in much of anything before meeting Gideon. But now she didn't know. Surely something bigger was happening here, if all this destiny, good versus evil stuff was to be true.

She was feathering through pages when some-

thing caught her eye. It was a picture of a large temple, built with pillars and gold embellishments. She stopped turning the pages when she saw the heading: Tabernacle at Shiloh.

Underneath the picture was a short paragraph about the location. There was a quote from the Bible, about how the tabernacle was a meeting place for the people of Israel. It was said to have housed the Ark of the Covenant. When Jude asked Gideon what that meant, he pulled up a chair next to her and looked at the page.

"Ah," he said, removing his glasses. He wiped the lenses off on his shirt and then put them back on. "The Ark of the Covenant is a chest. It's a heavy, golden box housing the stone tablets where Moses wrote down the Ten Commandments. Very sacred to the Hebrew people."

He slid the book closer to him. "This is the city of Shiloh. It was the capital of Israel before it was destroyed in a battle. The capitol was then moved to Jerusalem."

"What happened to the Ark?"

"No one really knows for sure. The Bible says that it was taken by the Philistines."

"Shiloh," she said to herself. She said it a few times aloud, gaging the taste of it on her tongue, the shape of it on her lips. It rolled off like soft butter and she liked the way it sounded. "What does it mean?" she asked.

Gideon looked surprised and confused. She'd asked him a question he couldn't answer. His Hebrew was not up to snuff. He stood and walked over to the bookshelf. He pulled a finger across the bindings until he came across a small, fat book entitled Hebrew Origins. He flipped through the pages until he found it. When he read it to himself, he smiled. He looked knowingly at Jude and said, "It means peace."

Jude looked down at the baby who was laying on some blankets on the floor, under one of those activity gyms, kicking at plastic ocean animals. "Shiloh," she said aloud. The baby looked right up at Jude, like she'd just been waiting for her to say it. Like it had been her name all along. Jude said it again, and she felt it rise up out of her, filling empty spaces and easing away confusion. Like something old and waiting, uncovered and released from the earth. She picked up the baby, picked up Shiloh, and knew, right then, that there was no question. Shiloh was her name: a name that meant something. A name that would remind her of who she was.

Shiloh!

Dirty, wearing a long, black dress, hair tangled, her eyes bloodshot. Shiloh, who was barely four years old. Shiloh, who was Jude's entire world. She was being dragged on a chain toward a fire by two hell beings. In that moment, Jude wanted nothing more than to rip their throats out with her own bare hands; to feel the tendons pop and spurt between her fingers as they fell to the ground. And she planned to.

CHAPTER 15

At first sight of Shiloh, Jude reacted. She threw the wheelbarrow into the vampires beside her and charged in the direction of her daughter. The fire inside of her was far more intense than the one blazing next to her.

The leader shouted and smashed his fist into the table. "What is going on here?" he screamed, spit flying out of his mouth. "Someone stop this!"

Ezra was running a few feet behind Jude when the vampires started crowding in.

"Don't let the child go! Bring her here! The consecrated one! She's the one we need!" The man began to chant in some ancient language. He hurried out from behind the table and sprinkled herbs into the fire. As he did, the flames changed from orange-red to green and silver.

Jude had crossed half the distance between her and Shiloh when she was intercepted by a vampire. It grabbed her around the neck and threw her back on the floor. From the ground, she caught a glimpse of Ezra who was fighting off attackers of her own. She quickly scanned for Christopher, but he was either already dead, or still disguised as one of them. While Jude was on the ground, three or four vampires piled on top of her, ripping at her skin. She thrusted her body upward as if defying gravity, but only for a moment. With a stake in hand, she pierced the heart of the vampire closest to her face. He turned to dust and she had to spit it out of her mouth. The other vampires closed in on her and she grabbed one by the neck of it's robe. With incomprehensible strength she threw him off of her and into the fire. There were others to take his place.

The man was still chanting. His chants were growing in intensity. He was raising his arms, eyes closed tightly. He screamed the words, refusing to look at the chaos around him. As if there was no hitch in his plan at all.

Drawing on strength from deep inside her that she didn't know she possessed, Jude lunged upward, forcing energy from the muscles in her back and her legs. She felt outside of herself. She threw punches and dodged and deflected, with speed and agility sourced from some previously untapped spring inside of herself. One vampire approached her and she punched him so hard in the gut that he fell back and stumbled into the flames. She pushed forward, and with every kill, she got closer to her daughter. She destroyed everything that stood in her way, laying waste to multiple at a time and leaving behind a trail of carnage and dust. With the dagger at her thigh she ripped through the neck of an assailant. She punctured the gut of another. She whipped out her crossbow and reloaded like mad, flinging arrows through the air at every being she could spot. She shot on sight, white hot rage fueling her rampage.

Jude pressed on, throwing the undead creatures into the fire and dropping others to their knees. For a split second, she glanced behind her at Ezra. For the first time since the fight began, she felt something other than rage. It was a hint of relief. Ezra was holding her own, on her feet and swinging her sword through the torsos of vampires at every turn.

As Jude was nearing Shiloh, the man's yelling reached its peak. His voice cracked and he screamed at the top of his lungs. The only words Jude could make out were “Come forth!”.

Jude was ten feet away from Shiloh. The air was now filled with the dust of the dead and her throat was dry. She coughed and her chest roared, gasping for air. The two demons still had Shiloh, one on each arm. They were dragging her toward the fire. Her feet would not leave the ground, but she was so small her resistance was nothing to them. She looked stoic, calm. She wasn’t crying, though it looked as if she had been. Jude’s heart hammered. Finally, almost instinctively, Shiloh glanced over at her and their eyes locked. Just like the first time their eyes ever met, there was a surge of electricity between them– an energy and connection almost palpable, holding fast to an unspoken promise, an incomprehensible bond that no force of hell could think of severing. Four eyes, glued together, deep, surging blue and reflecting the flames that licked their skin. "I'm coming for you!" Jude yelled, but her voice was muffled.

A horrible sound rose up from the fire, like stones grinding against one another. Jude turned toward the flame and saw it: a huge marble statue rose from the pit of the fire. Ezra had stopped fighting and was looking, too. It seemed all the chaos and violence in the stone room had come to a halt and all eyes were on the immense figure rising from the inferno.

It took Jude a moment to recognize it. It was massive, and the fire distorted her vision. But she narrowed her focus, saw through the flames, and knew exactly what it was. Molech. It had the head of a bull, and its mouth was open wide, ready to receive the sacrifice.

Behind the flame, behind the statue, Jude found Shiloh again. The two demons were dragging her toward the man with the book. When they reached him, he took Shiloh by the arms and pulled her toward him. She fought, thrusting her arms at him, but he was too strong. She couldn't break free.

Ezra, who had been a few yards to the right of Jude, bolted for Shiloh. Immediately, a horde of vampires was on her, but she stood her ground. For a moment she looked at Jude, and then to Shiloh, saying something with her eyes. She had created a diversion. Jude saw her opening, and she took it.

She ran, her legs springing from the stone floor as if they were filled with helium, toward Shiloh and the man. She gripped her dagger in her right hand, and plunged it through the bodies of every monster that got between her and her daughter. The man had begun pouring oil over her head. In a bowl next to him was blood, collected from God knew what, and he began to draw lines on Shiloh's forehead, using his finger for a brush, and the blood for paint. He spoke softly to her, whispering in another language.

When Jude got close enough to make out the man's face, and see the flecks of light in Shiloh's eyes, she reached out and grabbed the table where the man was sitting. He looked up at her, startled. He had been so engrossed in Shiloh that he had not seen Jude approaching. Jude looked him in the eyes and launched his table across the room, into the flame. The bowl of blood splattered across the floor and onto her shoes.

For a moment he looked at Jude in confusion. “Kill her!” he yelled finally. His voice rose above the fire and echoed off the walls. The two beasts who had been dragging Shiloh approached Jude with lust in their eyes. The largest of the two drug it's brown, rotting tongue across it's teeth and let out a short, shrill laugh. With Shiloh still in the grip of the angry man, Jude turned to the two demons. They were muscled, with protruding veins in their upper arms. They had dog-like teeth and snouts and nails that looked like polished steel. Her knuckles were white and locked around the handle of the dagger. She worried that it wouldn't be enough to vanquish whatever these twin demons were.

The two demons looked at each other and seemed to agree on something. Then the first one lunged. He came at her from the front while the other moved behind. Jude could hear his teeth clatter as he snapped at her neck. He seemed to transform into an animal, when before he had been humanesque in stature. His eyes seemed to darken. He had a deadly grip on Jude's arm and she fought him off with her other, gripping the dagger but unable to make it reach his body. She stabbed the toe of her shoe into his abdomen and he didn't flinch. She could feel her strength fading. With every snap of his jaw, Jude felt her arm going weak. She could smell his breath. Feel it's damp warmth on her skin. He was going to kill her.

Her arm began to tremble. She could barely stand; he was about to knock her to the ground. Once she hit the floor, Jude knew she would lose this fight. Images of Shiloh flashed through her mind. She couldn't see her. She couldn't turn her head. That man had her and he was going to kill her, too. Then what? Jude closed her eyes and yelled at the top of her lungs, expending every last bit of oxygen she had. Her knees were shaking so hard that she thought she was experiencing an earthquake. "Shiloh!" she yelled, eyes still closed. She had nothing more to say. Had no oxygen left to speak. She felt her back hit the ground, her shoulder blades digging into the stone. She refused to open her eyes. Her dagger lay on the ground beside her. She didn't bother looking for it. She only hoped that Shiloh wasn't watching.

The demon moved in on her. She had lost track of where the other one was, but it didn't matter. One was on top of her, its weight crushing her abdomen. She could feel its claws breaking the skin on her arm. Her head spun and she couldn't resist it. She had no strength to fight.

She felt the monsters head close in on her neck. She felt it lick her skin. Then she felt it sink it's teeth into her flesh.

CHAPTER 16

It must've been less than a second. She could hear the gushing, wet sound of blood and saliva mingling below her ear. But the next thing she felt was the release of weight. It seemed as if the demon had been struck with something and fallen back, releasing its grip on her body. Its face was no longer buried into Jude's neck. She heard a roar. Everything was black. Surely this was the end.

"Mama!" a small, familiar voice cried over the chaos. Jude knew she was dreaming. It was Shiloh, pulling her into the next life. "Mama!" the voice called again. "Please get up!"

Get up. In the darkness, Jude reconnected to the cold harsh stone under her body. "Get up!"

"Damnit, Jude, get up!" This was a different voice. Not Shiloh. Jude thrust her eyes open and woke up in hell, but very much alive.

She inhaled, and felt her organs reactivate, her heart racing, her lungs stiff and burning. She lifted her arms above her head and they seemed to float there, like balloons. They fell back at her side like jello.

"Get up!" Ezra called again, and Jude turned to look at her. She was holding a sword, crossbow at her feet. Behind her was Christopher. Jude had forgotten he'd existed. He clutched the cross in his hand and repeated something over and over–something that Jude recognized from a half-remembered Sunday school class. His voice was commanding, and he yelled to the demons. Sweat rolled from his hairline and he had removed his robe. He was breathing heavily, his chest heaving from the volume of his speech. His white shirt was soiled with coal dust and sweat, untucked, disheveled. But Christopher Alleghiri was more focused than Jude had ever seen him. His words seemed to deter and weaken the demons. It didn't kill them, but they were noticeably slowed. The other monster was clawing at her but kept its distance from the sharp blade of Ezra's sword, and the sting of Christopher's words.

"Jude, get up! Get Shiloh!" Ezra yelled.

Jude took rapid inventory of every part of her body, muscles twitching. Rebounded to her feet, she swiped the dagger from the floor. She scanned the room, and found Shiloh. The man had her by the collar of the black dress. He was pulling Shiloh toward the fire, toward the statue, still chanting, his eyes wild.

Again finding strength from thin air, Jude lurched at him. She reached him in seconds, her dagger sweeping a clean slice through his robe, ripping a slash through his chest.

For a second, he just stood there, teetering on the edge of his life. His eyes went dim and he looked down in a daze at the bleeding wound. He looked back at Jude, lifting his eyes slowly, thoughtfully. He pressed one hand on his chest, and reached the other toward Jude. Before she could respond at all, he fell to his knees. The jar of oil in his hand shattered on the stone floor, and he laid there, mangled and writhing.

Without thinking, Jude plunged her dagger through the open gash, and watched as the life flooded out of him. She felt his body go slack beneath the weight of her fist. Then she stood there for a second, confused, wondering at the humanity of his death. No dust. He was a man.

"Mama!" cried Shiloh.

Jude whipped her head around to the child standing with her toes on the edge of the fire pit. The vampires had all come to a pause as their leader gasped and died. Once he was gone, all eyes were on Jude, but this time, they were afraid.

One of the vampires standing near Shiloh darted out of the room, headed for the tunnel. With only one vampire left on Shiloh's arm, Jude dove in her direction. She ripped the vampire's hand away from her daughter, and as it tried to turn and run, she grabbed it by the neck and stabbed it in the chest. The ones who were still alive looked nervously around the room at one another, then all dropped their wheelbarrows and shovels and ran for the exit.

Shiloh stood behind her, still inches from the fire and seemingly unable to move. Jude flew to her, wrapped her arms around her tiny body and swept her away from the flames.

"Shiloh," she sobbed into her daughter's neck. "I'm so sorry. It's going to be okay. Everything's going to be okay now." Jude couldn't stop talking. Words fell out of her mouth, some of them senseless, and onto Shiloh's shoulder along with her tears. She sucked in the air around her deeply, taking in the scent of her daughter, dirty and exhausted but still Shiloh. Still alive. "It's going to be okay," she repeated. "I've got you now and I'll never let you go." Her arms encircled the child tighter than they ever had before. For a long time, they stayed like that, desperately holding onto each other. Jude could barely breathe. Powerful sobs racked her body. She knew that she was losing a lot of blood from her neck and other wounds all over, but she could do nothing more than hold Shiloh and whisper hundreds, thousands of thank-yous to Heaven. Minutes passed and Ezra came up and tapped Jude on the shoulder. Jude opened her eyes for the first time, and saw Ezra standing with her back to the flame. "Hey," she whispered, kneeling down beside them. She ran her hand over Shiloh's back and gave her a kiss on the top of her head. "We gotta go," she whispered calmly. "They might come back.. And we have to get to a hospital."

Jude looked Ezra up and down and saw that her arms were bloodied, and her face was bruised. Christopher was scratched up and was bleeding slowly from a bite on the back of his hand, but was otherwise unharmed. “You’re not looking too great either,” she said, looking over Shiloh for any sign of injury. There was a small cut on the palm of her hand, but other than that she seemed okay.

“Yeah, well, we all need some help,” answered Ezra.

Ezra pulled Jude to her feet, but Jude wouldn’t let go of Shiloh. Despite her extreme weakness and the pain that was now radiating through her entire body, Jude placed Shiloh on her hip and refused to put her down. When she got to her feet, she looked around the filthy battleground.

Memory struck Jude like a ton of bricks. “Samantha and Lacey,” she said weakly, her energy rebuilding at the thought of them. She had been so intent on saving Shiloh that she had all but forgotten about them. “They’re in here someplace,” she asserted. “We can’t leave without them.”

Christopher approached Shiloh and brushed her hair away from her tear-soaked eyes. “You’re going to be okay,” he told her sweetly. “Did you see any other little girls in here?”

Shiloh shook her head ‘yes’. “They’re in the waiting room,” she answered. “Right down the hall.”

"We'll go," said Christopher. "You sit here and catch your breath."

Jude immediately agreed, and slid down against the wall to sit with Shiloh in her lap.

Not five minutes later, Christopher and Ezra returned, each with a tired, tattered girl in their arms. They had been down in the furnace for days. Jude pulled herself up with Shiloh on her hip, walked to them and pulled them both toward her for a hug.

"It's alright," said Jude. "You are going to be okay now." The girls were sobbing, and obviously dehydrated and terrified, but except for marks on their palms, just like Shiloh, they were unharmed.

Jude looked at Ezra and they both looked around the room. The body of the man Jude had killed was still there on the ground, mouth open, in a pool of blood.

"Don't think about it, Jude," said Ezra sternly. "Let's get out of here."

When they emerged from the furnace, it was dark. The woods were calm and cool, and Jude collapsed onto the leaves. "Just for a minute," she said, exasperated. Shiloh sat down against Jude's side, and they sat on the forest floor, breathing deeply and trying to muster the strength to make it to the truck.

Samantha and Lacey sat down beside Jude and Shiloh, and Jude smiled at them. "Everyone has been worried about you two," she said between breaths, with her hand resting over her stomach as it rose and fell, the waves getting smaller with each breath. "Your parents are going to be so happy you're okay."

She could barely hold her eyes open, and her voice was cracked and fading. Still, she made sure both of them felt secure. "We're going to get in the truck and take you two to the hospital where your parents will come for you. Does that sound good?"

They both nodded fervently and Jude took one more moment to savor the simple feeling of being alive. She had never taken the time to really appreciate it before. The leaves beneath her back crunched, and frogs and cicadas could be heard milling about the night forest. Looking straight up, she could see the dark shadows of branches against the pale blue sky. Through them, a few scattered stars blinked. Most importantly, warm fingers wrapped around her own, and she could hear Shiloh's slow, steady breath, feel her pulse, smell her hair. Everything was going to be okay. Reluctantly, she stood up again. "Good," she said, scooping Shiloh back up. "Let's go."

By the time they had climbed the hillside to the truck, Jude was ready to collapse. Samantha and Lacey were out of breath, their little legs unable to go any further. Christopher, who had remained in the best condition, helped everyone into the truck. Ezra sat in the bed with Samantha and Lacey and Jude and Shiloh rode in the cab.

On the way down the mountain, Jude's body finally began to surrender to the trauma of the day. She started to fade in and out, and Christopher kept talking to her, trying to force her consciousness. Jude was struggling to focus and to keep her eyes open. She held her hand over the wound in her neck, but could feel warm blood draining and running down her arm. Her body had been pushed to the limit, then shoved over it.

"Just a little longer," Christopher kept saying.

Shiloh sat in the middle seat, pressed airtight against Jude's side, her eyes closed the entire time. She occasionally whispered something, but Christopher couldn't make it out.

"Shiloh, honey, are you alright?" he asked, but Shiloh never opened her eyes. She kept moving her hands. She would place them on Jude's lap for a minute or two, then move them to her arms. Finally, she laid her whole body down over Jude, with both arms around her mother's neck, and a leg on either side, and looked like she had fallen asleep.

Christopher pulled the truck up to the ambulance bay of Acadia Hospital and opened the passenger door. Jude would have fallen onto the pavement if not for her seatbelt. Shiloh sat up and opened her eyes. "Are we at the hospital?" she asked.

"Yeah, but everything's going to be alright," Ezra told her, helping Samantha and Lacey out of the truck bed. Christopher lifted Shiloh from the cab and planted her on the pavement at his side. Carefully, he unbuckled Jude and caught her as her limp body slid from the seat. Ezra pulled all three girls close and waited until Jude was safely out of the truck to move toward the building.

An orderly in blue scrubs ran out of the automatic glass doors and toward them. "You can't leave this truck here," he insisted. "It's for the ambulance!"

His eyes fell on Jude and the three little girls. "Oh my God," he gasped. "Hold on!"

He ran back inside and reappeared moments later with a gurney and two other trauma doctors. Several nurses followed them out to see the spectacle.

"We need to get her on the table," said one of the doctors, pointing at Jude. "Are these the girls from the news?"

"Yes," Ezra said weakly, as the doctors and nurses scrambled to get everyone into the building. "Call their parents. Everyone here needs to see a doctor right away. They've been through hell, trust me."

With that, Ezra passed out into the arms of an orderly.

CHAPTER 17

Jude opened her eyes to a sterile white room. She had a needle in her arm with a tube that led to a bag filled with some clear liquid. She sat up and found herself in a hospital, her head throbbing. Her left arm was in a heavy cast, and she had bandages all over her body. Another cast wrapped up her right foot and ankle. Her chest was heavy and tight, and her breath was labored.

Her thoughts came back to her and she started remembering the events of the past . . . was it days? Hours? She had no idea how long she'd been out. And Shiloh. Last she'd seen her little girl, she was dirty and scared and hurt.

"Hey!" she yelled loudly, ignoring the call button on the plastic arm of the bed. "Somebody, I need to talk to somebody!"

As she reached for the IV tube to pull it from her arm, she felt a hand over her own. "You're awake," Christopher said, in a tender voice. He sat in a chair that looked too small for him, scooted up to her bedside. He looked tired, like he'd been there for a long time.

Jude was about to answer when two nurses came rushing into the room. They came near her bed and started adjusting monitors and recording data.

"How do you feel, Jude?" asked a bubbly nurse in Winnie the Pooh scrubs.

"Where's Shiloh?" Jude asked. "I want to see my daughter. Is she okay? Where is she?"

The other nurse put her hand on Jude's arm. "She's fine," she said softly. "She's doing great. She was dehydrated, and had a small cut on her head, and one on her palm that was getting infected. But Dr. Calvert put her on some antibiotics and stitched up her head and she's alert and has been asking for you."

Jude exhaled. "I want to see her. Can I see her?"

"Sure!" The nurse promptly turned and disappeared into the hallway.

"Is she going to get Shiloh?" Jude asked the other nurse.

"Yes she is," she answered warmly. "You are going to be quite the celebrity. The whole town is waiting to hear your account of the story. Lacey and Samantha's parents want to personally thank you."

"How are they?" Jude asked. "Are they okay?"

The nurse smiled. "You saved their lives. They're going to be fine."

"And Ezra? Where is Ezra?"

"Your friend?" asked the nurse. "Oh, she was released this morning. But I think she is still here. She's been with Shiloh since she could get out of bed."

The door opened and the other nurse returned, holding Shiloh in her arms. Shiloh smiled wide, and Jude threw her head back on the pillow and closed her eyes as relief flooded her body.

The nurse put Shiloh on the floor and she immediately ran to her mother.

"Be careful," said the nurse as the little girl climbed onto the bed.

Jude gave Shiloh a tight hug. "Boy am I glad to see you," she whispered. "Are you alright?"

Shiloh nodded. "They gave me green jello!"

Jude laughed and pulled Shiloh onto the pillow next to her. "I thought I lost you," said Jude, refusing the tear that threatened to spill out of her eye.

Shiloh put her head down on Jude's chest and closed her eyes. She was still exhausted, and according to the nurse, unwilling to sleep in the hospital. She wanted Jude, and as soon as they were reunited, the child fell quickly and deeply asleep.

The nurse moved away from the door, and two people more came into the room. First, Ezra, on crutches.

Jude grimaced. "Oh, no," she said. "I'm sorry."

Ezra laughed. "Yeah, well, I think I'm better off than you."

Jude shrugged as best she could, wrapped in bandages and tubes. "Thank you," she said earnestly. "Both of you." Christopher reached out for her hand and she wrapped her fingers around his. "Without you guys, I don't know if-"

"Doesn't matter," Ezra cut her off. "We were there and we all made it."

Jude ran her hand through Shiloh's hair as she slept on her chest. The hospital room door opened again, and in came a welcomed, familiar face.

Gideon. Tall, dressed in an army green pull over and baseball cap, his white beard groomed closely to his face and plaid shirt tucked into his blue jeans.

Jude lifted her head from the pillow as he walked over to the bed. "What are you doing here?" she asked.

"Ezra called me and told me what happened. She said you were pretty beat up." It didn't even matter what he was saying. His voice brought calm.

He stood there, scanning her, looking nervously at the monitors and tubes.

"I'll be fine," Jude said casually, reaching out to touch his arm. "You should see the other guy."

He looked at her and smiled. "I'm glad you're alright."

"How long have I been in here?" she asked anyone who would answer.

"You were out for about a day," answered Ezra.

Gideon sat down on the stool in the corner and wheeled it over to the crowd. The nurse checked all of Jude's vitals, and found them to be where they should be.

"Now," she said with excitement. "There are police officers and a camera crew waiting outside to talk to you. They all want to get the story of how you three saved Lacey and Samantha."

Ezra looked at Jude. "I didn't want to say anything to anyone until you were awake."

Jude nodded. "I don't want to say anything to anyone at all."

She glanced at Gideon, who understood, and nodded in affirmation.

"We'll talk to the cops if we have too," said Jude. "But I don't want any names in the paper or on the news."

"I think the whole town already knows who you are," said the nurse, timidly.

"Not surprising," said Jude.

"I'll take care of it," said Gideon, standing and moving for the door. "Don't worry about any of it."

Three days later, Jude walked out of the hospital, or rather rolled out, with a broken ankle, broken arm, fractured wrist, three bruised ribs, and forty-six stitches spread out over multiple cuts and contusions all over her body. She had a swollen lip, a black eye, and had slept off a fairly serious concussion in the hospital. She was in a lot of pain, and on a lot of meds, but in a few days, maybe weeks, she would be fine.

Shiloh had five stitches, done in purple per her request, but was otherwise unscathed. Jude had a difficult time keeping Shiloh from rubbing her fingers over the bumpy thread. But being four, and being Shiloh were both mercies for which Jude could not be more grateful. The child seemed to have recovered all but entirely from the experience, which could easily leave anyone traumatized.

The police came and took a report. Jude told them that Shiloh had been taken by the driver of the black SUV. She told the police that she found Shiloh by following it into the mountains. She said that when she arrived, she found a man who appeared to be performing some kind of ritual and that he must've been a part of some kind of cult. They must have known there was more to the story. Maybe they didn't ask because they knew it was more than they could handle. The Synedrion had already swept the case clean. Authorities in the state police department were briefed, meaning they were given a false story clearing Jude's name of any records. With power extending all the way up to the most secured documentation in Washington DC, Jude was unworried that she would face any repercussions.

She told the officer that she killed the man. They went back for the body, and that was that. She had to sign some papers. Nothing ever came of it. He was from out of town, and had no relatives. His name was Jim Hopkins. He really was a part of some cult. But he was also a man. A man that Jude had killed. He wasn't supernatural, and didn't turn to dust. He wasn't inherently evil. Or maybe he was. But he was a man.

"I killed him," she told Gideon, sitting at the breakfast table on her first morning home while everyone else was asleep. "I killed a person."

She wasn't devastated, but she thought maybe she should be.

Gideon sipped his coffee. "Jude," he said calmly. "I've been to war, and I've carried a gun, knowing that if I had to, I would use it to take a life. But only a life that threatened mine. War is a terrible thing, but it happens," he said. He took another sip and turned the page of the newspaper in front of him. "I've taken a life. And I've watched men die. It changes you. But you have a calling."

He always had this hard-boiled way of speaking, of thinking. Things were black and white. The ends justified the means.

But Jude felt a twinge of guilt, even against his reassurance. Anyone else in her situation would face a trial, a ruling, maybe jail time. "My calling isn't to kill people. I'm not a vigilante."

"You are," said Gideon, without a moment's pause. "That's exactly what you are. You serve a different kind of justice. One that the law will never be able to handle."

Jude shook her head. Her neck was still sore and the bandage caught her hair.

"I'm not saying that gives you a license to kill," said Gideon. "But you're fighting a war. You do what you have to do to win it. You eliminate the enemy, no matter what form they come in. That man was going to raise Molech. He was going to sacrifice Shiloh to do it. And the hell that would've been unleashed afterwards would've killed many more."

"I wonder how many other demons could be awakened by Shiloh's blood."

Gideon shrugged. "Probably a lot. Your blood could probably awaken a few demons as well. But we're not going to let that happen."

Jude accepted his answer. She had to. She wasn't one to dwell on the past. She killed a man, but that man was going to kill her daughter. She was shaken by the event. There was an uncomfortable knot in the pit of her stomach, and thinking about it sometimes made her head spin, but she was not so distraught that she couldn't function. She knew that others in this situation would be. It was then, maybe, that she discovered the real difference between her and Shiloh. Sweet, gentle Shiloh was the spirit of human innocence. She was purity and all things good. Jude knew in her heart that in order to protect something so sacred, with a righteous fire that the world would be so anxious to extinguish, she would have to reject that kind of status. In order to protect what is right and good and blameless, Jude must be faulted, reactive, and often guilty. She must be able to make choices, to value the life of Shiloh over all others. Whether this was an attribute of her destiny, or simply the naked reality of parenthood, she was unsure. But she had always been capable of those qualities. Until now they had been untested, laying dormant. The content of her character had not changed since Shiloh, but rather, it had adapted. Things she no longer needed fell by the wayside, and other things took their place. Apathy was replaced with passion. Listlessness with vigilance. Fear with action. Anger with vengeance. She realized that without first thinking about it, she had done it. She had killed a man to save her daughter, and she knew in her gut that she would do it again. She searched her heart for some kind of moral objection to her rationale, but found nothing.

Ezra hobbled into the kitchen on her crutches and said good morning. Gideon stood up and patted Jude gently on the back. "I'm gonna go watch cartoons with the kid," he said, making his way to the living room where Shiloh was watching Scooby Doo and eating Cheerios. Ezra slumped down into the chair he had been sitting in. "Ugh," she groaned. "Why is the coffee so damn far away."

Jude stood up, carefully got her balance on her wobbly, pained legs and poured her a cup.

"You didn't have to do that," said Ezra, as Jude handed it to her.

Jude sat back down and shrugged and watched Ezra take a sip. "I heal faster than most," she said. "Movement is good for me."

Quiet fell over the breakfast table as Ezra drank her coffee and Jude watched with a grin.

"What?" asked Ezra, looking up from the mug.

"You're a badass," said Jude.

Ezra looked away. "What are you talking about?"

"You know what I'm talking about," said Jude. "You roll in here all sweet and innocent, with your classical education and your wealth of supernatural knowledge. I'm thinking you'll be useful as an encyclopedia, sure, but not much more." She paused.

"But I was wrong." Jude wasn't one for expressions of emotion. "You had my back," she said. "You held your own. You saved my life. And Shiloh's life."

Ezra felt heat rising around her neck. "No, I-"

"You did," insisted Jude. "I wouldn't be here without you."

Ezra looked up and smiled. "Well," she said, definitively. "That's why I'm here."

Jude nodded. "I'm glad you are."

CHAPTER 18

Shiloh was fully recovered as soon as she got home. Nothing could shake that child's sunny disposition. Nothing. She was happy to be back in her own house, happy to see Gideon, and happy to know that her mom was going to be alright. Five days had passed since they all came home from the hospital and Shiloh had been patiently waiting for life to pick back up again. It was a sunny day, the kind that children simply cannot resist, and Gideon had promised her ice cream.

He was to fly back to Indiana in the morning, and Shiloh was already missing him, begging him to stay. The ice-cream was an attempt at placating the little girl, and it was working. By lunchtime, she was so excited to go into town that she had tied her own shoes, put on her jacket and was standing by the door. Everyone else moved a little more slowly, Ezra still on crutches and Jude a little achy all over, with bandages wrapping her midsection and her ankle, but they powered through the pain, and climbed in the car. It was worth the effort just to see Shiloh excited over something so simple, like any other kid would be.

It was a typical Saturday mid-morning in town. The farmer's market was bustling with shoppers, and all the storefronts were looking their best, doors open with hand-painted *Open* signs hanging from brass knobs.

They strolled down Main Street, with Shiloh in Gideon's arms. Ezra managed well with her crutches, determined to not let a little pain slow her down. The warm ache around Jude's ribs was the worst of all of her injuries, but the autumn sun felt good on her shoulders, and the air was refreshing and smelled like funnel cake and freshly cut grass. She knew that it would only take a few days to be back at full strength, and getting back to normal life would help the healing process. When they turned into the farmer's market to find lunch, Shiloh saw puppies for sale and begged to go pet them.

The litter was running around, tripping over one another in a small pen in the back of someone's pick-up truck. They were cute puppies, some kind of hound dog, with short copper fur and long ears.

"Mama, can I please have one?" she begged, her hands folded at her chest like an angel. In the sunlight, her big eyes beamed and her feathery hair blew over her shoulders and behind her on the wind. Jude loved the way her face lit up, admired her smile, the shape of her lips curling up, her pink cheeks filling up to the bottoms of her eyes. Jude exhaled, suddenly weakened.

“Shiloh,” she said reluctantly. “I don’t know.” But already, she could feel herself giving in.

The girl turned around and scratched one of the puppies on the head, her little fingers playing over the puppy's ears.

A teenage girl sitting on the tailgate of the truck smiled at Shiloh and offered to let her climb into the pen. She sat, beyond delighted, on the pickup tailgate surrounded by puppies and Jude worried she’d end up going home with all of them. One of the puppies had a small tuft of white fur under his belly and climbed right into Shiloh’s lap. He put his head down on her knees and let out a big yawn. Shiloh leaned down and kissed him on the head, picked him up and carried him like she carried her dolls, laying over her arms, to Jude.

“This is the one I love most,” she announced. “And he loves me too.”

The puppy hadn’t moved or squirmed or made a peep. He was resting his lazy head over her arm, completely content. It did seem as though they had found each other by design.

The teenage girl smiled. “He’s my favorite, too,” she told Shiloh. “He’s really sweet, and he loves to have his ears scratched.”

Shiloh scratched behind his droopy ears. “I’ll take good care of him,” she promised.

The girl looked at Jude. “She’s sweet,” she said. “I think she needs a puppy.”

Jude let out a willing sigh and nodded at Shiloh. “Alright,” she said. “You can have him.”

Shiloh threw one arm around Jude’s legs, said thank-you, then hugged the puppy, the one she loved the most, and carried him all over town.

“What are you going to name him?” asked Ezra.

Shiloh looked up, thrilled with the idea of endowing the puppy with a name. She smiled wide. “Um,” she said, contemplating her options. “I think I’ll name him Jack.”

“I like it,” Jude said, taking Shiloh by the hand. The puppy snuggled against her chest in her other arm.

A vendor at the market was selling hot dogs and barbecue out of a truck, and it was decided that they would take a lunch break. Since she had opened her eyes in the hospital, Jude was starving. Her body, uniquely tailored to endure physical abuse and to recover quickly, was in search of all the energy it could get. They were sitting down at a picnic table in the shade of a Sycamore tree to eat when Jude was tapped on the shoulder.

She turned, startled.

"Hey," said Christopher, standing awkwardly behind her, towering above her as he did.

"Hey," she answered back, hotdog in hand. She hadn't seen him since the hospital, but she learned from Ezra that Christopher was there the whole time, moving back and forth between Jude and Shiloh, but mostly sitting at Jude's bedside, waiting for her to wake up, checking with doctors and nurses, monitoring her as she slept. Things were different with him, as one might expect after sharing a near-death experience involving unmentionable hell-beings in an ancient furnace. He seemed more still, less nervous. He smiled at her gently, and she waited for one of them to speak.

Finally, he cleared his throat. "It's good to see you here," he said. "Must mean you're feeling better."

Jude smiled gratefully. "Thanks," she answered. "Yeah, much better. I think we all are."

He scanned her up and down. The silver scar on her head from where she'd hit the rearview mirror in the accident caught and reflected the light of the early afternoon. "Good."

"Yeah..." Jude said again, sensing the tension of unspoken words.

"Hey, Christopher!" Shiloh squealed. She stood and gave him a hug, leaving the puppy on the picnic table. Then she grabbed him by the hand and pulled him toward her seat. "Look what mom just got me!" She scooped the puppy up and held it out toward him.

Christopher accepted with a huge smile and scratched his belly.

"His name's Jack," Shiloh told him.

He laughed. "I had a dog named Jack when I was a kid. He was a good dog."

"Well, you can play with him whenever you want," she told him.

His face became softer, his eyes more tender. He took one of Shiloh's tiny hands in his. "I'm so glad that you're okay," he told her quietly. "You are a very special little girl. I think someday, the whole world is going to know that."

He handed Jack back to Shiloh and looked to Jude. "Maybe you and I could talk sometime," he said. "Maybe over coffee? I know it would help me make sense of things."

Jude nodded. "Of course," she answered.

"Great," he said softly. He nodded politely to Gideon and Ezra, tucked his hands back into the pockets of his slacks, and disappeared into the market crowd.

CHAPTER 19

Later that day, after Shiloh's belly had been stuffed with ice cream, Gideon and Ezra both decided to take an afternoon nap. Despite the pain ricocheting through her body, Jude was too wired to rest. It had been nearly a week since they found the girls in the old furnace and stopped the ritual that would raise Molech from hell, but since then, Jude had barely slept. She spent her nights in the hospital watching television reruns and researching demons on the internet. Her first night at home, she tried to sleep. She put Shiloh down in the bed next to her, tickled her back until she fell asleep, then tried to sleep herself, but couldn't. Her mind was racing, replaying the scenes from the cave over and over; an endless critique of her performance. She watched it like a DVD on repeat in her brain and judged what she did well, what she could have done better. She was amazed, after walking around all afternoon with Gideon and Ezra, that she was still standing, but she was remarkably awake. Her body was working double overtime to heal itself, and she'd expected that to be draining. Instead, it seemed to give her extra energy.

While Gideon and Ezra napped, Jude scrubbed the kitchen like she never had before. She cleaned the windows, mopped the floors, even lined the drawers with newspaper.

Shiloh sat by the back door, looking out the glass window with Jack in her arms. It had been agonizingly sunny, and Shiloh had been reluctant to go home after the ice-cream trip.

Jude stood at the sink washing dishes. Above the sink was a window through which she could see the entire backyard. It was a beautiful day. Crisp and bright. The sun pierced vividly through a thin sheet of white clouds, and reflected off the Autumn leaves, casting an orange-washed glow over everything. Winter would be coming soon. Jude knew that these days were numbered.

Shiloh had been begging to go outside, but gave up after being told "no" about fifteen times. Jude was starting to feel bad. Was she going to be like this forever? Afraid of the light of day because bad things existed? The most pressing "bad thing" was gone. Jude killed it herself. Shiloh deserved the chance to have fun, to play outside like a normal kid.

She looked down at Shiloh, desperate for a little fresh air. "Alright," she said reluctantly. "You can play outside for a few minutes."

Shiloh bounced, her feet lifting from the floor with a cheer and threw her arms around Jude's legs. Then she ran upstairs. Less than a minute later, she returned wearing a light blue jacket, and carrying a backpack full of toys in one arm, and Jack in the other.

He hung from her arm happily, his fuzzy ears sagging over his eyes.

Jude zipped Shiloh's jacket and walked with her onto the back porch. She pointed out landmarks in the yard and created an invisible fence. "Don't go past that tree. Don't go beyond the driveway. Stay on this side of the shed."

Shiloh eagerly agreed to all of Jude's stipulations.

"I'll be watching from the window," Jude told her.

Shiloh nodded and gave Jude another hug. Then she went bouncing off the porch and into the crunchy, yellowing grass. Jude stayed on the porch for a few minutes, but the wind began to blow and she was cold without a jacket. Everything seemed calm, so she went back to the dishes.

Five minutes had passed and Shiloh had been happily playing in the yard. Jude was scrubbing a large pot when the sponge slipped out of her hand. She bent down to pick it up. It couldn't have been more than fifteen seconds. She was slow moving and her bruised ribs grabbed at her as she bent. She stood back up, looked out the window, and Shiloh was gone.

Jude threw the sponge in the sink and left the water running. "Shiloh!" She yelled, bursting through the back porch screen door and into the harsh sunlight. She looked all over and didn't see Shiloh.

"Shiloh, where are you?" she called, but there was no answer. She turned back towards the house to wake Gideon, in sheer panic, already sweating and breathing heavily. Then she saw a lump under the kitchen window. Shiloh sat facing the brick of the house, hunched over on her knees. Jude ran to her. "Shiloh, why didn't you answer me?" she asked, agitated.

Shiloh didn't answer.

Jude put her hand on Shiloh's shoulder and knelt beside her. "Shi, what are you-"

Shiloh was holding something, cradling it close to her chest. The puppy sat calmly by her side, chewing on the dead grass.

"What is that?"

Shiloh's eyes were closed and she was mumbling quietly to herself. Jude gently pulled Shiloh's hand back, and saw that the child was cradling a dead cardinal.

"Oh, Shiloh, don't touch that!" Jude insisted. "Honey, it's dead, and very dirty."

Shiloh was catatonic, refusing to open her eyes or let go of the bird.

"Shiloh, are you okay? Talk to me." Jude was about to scream for Gideon, panicking.

Then, Shiloh opened her eyes with a smile. She put one finger over her mouth and said, "Shhh." With the other hand, she lifted the bird towards the sky.

"Shiloh, sweetheart," Jude whispered. "The bird can't fly. He's-"

Jude thought she was seeing things when it's wings began to ruffle. Suddenly the bird perked up and stood to its feet in Shiloh's palm.

"Go on," said Shiloh. "Fly away."

Jude sat back on her heels and rubbed her hand over her eyes. She watched the bird until she couldn't see it anymore, then stared blankly at the spot where it had disappeared.

Shiloh stood up, brushed the dirt from her knees, and slapped her hands against her skinny legs, a call which the puppy had already learned and answered to. He stood to his wobbly feet and followed her back into the house in no particular hurry. "Are you coming, mama?" asked Shiloh as she pulled open the screen door. It clattered behind her and Shiloh was gone, leaving Jude breathless on the ground.

Once Jude came to her senses she stumbled to the kitchen, still scanning the sky for the bird. Shiloh was sitting at the table sharing a pack of saltine crackers with Jack and coloring in a coloring book. Jude looked at her in confusion before moving to the bottom of the stairs.

"Gideon, you'd better come down here!" she called, keeping one eye on Shiloh and trying to disguise the mystification in her voice.

About two minutes later, Gideon emerged, still sleepy from his nap. "Is something wrong?" he asked from the top of the stairs.

"Uh," answered Jude slowly. "Honestly, I have no idea."

They stood in the living room, where Shiloh couldn't hear, joined by Ezra.

"What's going on?" Gideon asked, looking around the house for any sign of danger.

"Well," Jude said, dry-mouthed. "So I was outside with Shiloh. She found a dead bird. She was hugging it and talking to it and I told her to put it down, but-"

"But what?" asked Gideon, when Jude stopped speaking.

"But, it flew away."

"The dead bird flew away?" asked Ezra, skeptically.

Jude nodded, still dumbfounded.

"Are you sure it was dead?" asked Gideon.

Jude gave a confident nod. "Yeah. Gideon, it was dead. It was missing feathers. It's eyes were closed, beak was hanging open. It was way dead."

"Hm," he answered casually. "Interesting."

"Interesting?" asked Jude.

Ezra stepped forward. "Well, it seems crazy but won't she have . . . powers?"

Gideon gave a slight nod and ran a hand through his thin, graying hair. "Yes, in a manner of speaking," he replied. "It is expected that the chosen one will display some level of supernatural capability. Healing has historically been one of those things."

"Right, but she's four," answered Jude. "She's only four. Shouldn't she be older? I mean, right now, she doesn't even know who she is. She thinks she's a regular kid."

"It will certainly make dissection day in bio class interesting," said Ezra with a smirk.

They all took a step toward the kitchen and watched Shiloh as she talked to Jack and scribbled with her whole fist wrapped around the crayons. She still wore her blue coat with the hood pulled up, zipped up to her neck. She was singing the puppy a song. She was carrying on as if nothing unusual had happened.

Jude leaned against the wall and crossed her arms over her chest, unable to peel her eyes away from Shiloh. "What do we do?" she asked earnestly.

"Well," whispered Gideon. "I guess we'd better let her in on the secret."

Want to find out what happens next?

The second book in the *Keeping Shiloh* series is called *Keeping Shiloh: Awakening*, and it's available on Amazon! Go check it out!

Reviews are gold to authors! If you enjoyed this book, please consider visiting Amazon and GoodReads to rate and review!

Also, don't forget to follow me on Twitter
@AMeyer_Writes

And on Facebook on the *Keeping Shiloh* fan page
@AMeyerAuthor

Thanks so much for reading!!

- A Meyer